THE PLUMED SERPENT

THE PLUMED SERPENT

RICHARD BARRY

ILLUSTRATIONS BY
ROGER B. MORRISON

COVER BY
HOWARD BROWN

POPULAR PUBLICATIONS · 2023

TABLE OF CONTENTS

THE PLUMED SERPENT

*Rorek the Red, fearless Viking from
distant Greenland, threw the ancient
Mayan empire into confusion when
he neared the shores of Yucatan*

PROLOGUE

"THE GUM CHEWERS of America have gnawed their way into a great story," said a Chicago gum magnate who had just come in from the Yucatan jungle, where he had been hiring native hunters of the chicle tree. This was in a hotel in Belize, Honduras.

"Do you mean those Mayan discoveries?" I asked.

"Yes," replied the gum man. "No white man could find those old ruins, but our demand for chicle, the base of all chewing gum, has induced the natives to push on into the jungle, and these natives have uncovered for the scientists the great finds at Chichen Itza, Uxmal, and other points. Thus the American habit of chewing gum has given us our knowledge that a civilization as marvelous as that of the Greeks existed on this continent before Columbus came."

"Are any Mayans living to-day?"

"Certainly. I have seen them myself."

"Could I see them and talk to them?"

The chicle chief demurred. "You might see them," he replied, "but I don't know about talking to them. As a rule, the real Mayan won't talk to a white man."

"Take me to them," I insisted.

So two weeks later we stopped before a hut on the banks of a sluggish river in Yucatan.

"There," said the gummer, "lives a Guarani Indian from Costa Rica. He is married to a Mayan woman. She won't talk to you, but he may."

I told the Guarani I wanted to hire him. He and his family had nothing to eat, so I thought my offer would interest him, but he seemed unenthusiastic; he feared I wanted him to go to work. But when I told him all I wanted him to do was to talk, we quickly struck a bargain.

The Guarani was a barbarian, an outlander to Maya, but he had married into the ancient Mayan aristocracy, and the pride of this position was such that it placed him above all necessity for work except begging and talking.

The children—a swarm; mostly there seemed to be only seven, but once I thought I counted eleven—were miserable, stunted, wasted creatures, who got a piece of chicken once a month, and corn for a week or two in the fall. The rest of the time they lived by eating the earth scooped from behind the hut where the chickens and pigs wallowed.

THE WIFE WAS a weazened little figure, about four feet eight inches in height, and no more than seventy pounds in weight. Her breasts and hips were flat, and her face almost devoid of intelligence. Her hands were rough and knotted with work and dirt. She had but two points indicating breeding—an exquisite nostril and a finely arched, exceedingly small foot.

As I looked on her my eye saw beyond—along the unbroken line of descent, a thousand years and more, to the days when her ancestors were masters of time and fate, builders of mighty cities, readers of the stars, computers of the equinox, lords of a great people, governors of the earth, and enjoyers of pomp and luxury.

In the princess there was something of stone;
and something of the rattlesnake

Then one day she smiled at me—just a little.

"I tell her," the Guarani explained, "you are from the home country of Quetzalcoatl."

"Say it again."

He pronounced it, syllable by syllable, "Quet-zal-co-á-tl."

Not so hard that way. "Who was he?" I asked.

"The greatest chief in all Maya, and the first Emperor of the Toltecs."

"But I come from farther away than Mexico."

"So did Quetzalcoatl!" replied the Guarani. "He came from beyond the seas. He is a white man—a god!"

This might be something interesting. "Tell me about Quetzalcoatl," I requested.

He shook his head. It was a buried secret. It had never been intrusted to written document, or to the hieroglyphs of the carved stone. The story had existed for nearly a thousand years, passed from one generation of Mayans to another. It could not be told to an outsider.

I went to my second pack donkey, undid the saddle-bags, and brought in half a dozen cakes of chocolate, some tins of milk, several cuts of pemmican, and dried nuts and fruits. That afternoon we feasted royally, and the wife of the Guarani presided at the head of the board. It was their first real meal in years; perhaps the first in their lives. I offered to buy them some land—which cost three pesos an acre.

She talked—aside to her husband. Later he sought me, alone, in my pup tent by the bank of the river.

"She says tell you all," the Guarani announced. "You are of the royal line—the noble breed—descended direct from Quetzalcoatl. Peace be on you under our roof. You are one of us."

Thus, in the weeks that followed, in the wasted lands of the forgotten empire, I listened to the throbbing saga of daring and romance.

The scientists are obliged to reconstruct a civilization from a few stray fragments of pottery and crumbling stone. The writer performs a similar task with halting and badly interpreted syllables in a rambling tongue.

But here is the story, as the Guarani relayed it to me from the ancient lips of his Mayan wife.

1

GODS ON THE WATERS

ON A MORNING in the month of Yaxkin—the Ewe—the seventh of the eighteen months of the Mayan calendar—a peccary scout in the entourage of the sister of the Emperor Za Ramna, peering through the reeds on the low shore of the sea now known as the Caribbean, was halted by a sight so startling that he stood for a long time as if transfixed.

To him it appeared that a clump of trees was riding upon the face of the great waters. It was a compact clump like a house, yet above it waved a huge banner, marvelous as the sacrificial banner which floated over the mighty red palace at Chichen Itza.

In this floating mirage—all too solid, too real, to be a dream—he saw the forms of men; enormous men, much larger than any he had ever seen before in the world of Maya. Giants. They were waving and shouting.

Suddenly he collapsed on his face in the sand as the true import of what he saw burst on his childlike mind. These must be gods. He abased himself in abject worship.

After a long time of prostration, during which he momentarily expected either to die or to be transported alive and whole into the heavens, he dared look again.

Now he saw the floating trees being tossed fiercely by

the waves. Up and down, in and out, approaching, but never reaching the shore. Evidently the surf was no respecter of these gods.

The seeker of peccary recovered sufficiently to rise and withdraw safely behind the reeds. To his surprise, nothing happened. There was no malign visitation from the divine visitors. Whereupon he bolted back to camp.

Shortly thereafter, in the royal presence of the princess, the awed scout related his unbelievable tale. At once the regal personage, who had already reached the advanced age of thirty-five and who was accustomed to being obeyed, ordered the captain of her personal archers to take an escort of palace guards, clothed in full armor, and armed with ceremonial spear and arrow, to reconnoiter, and report.

The Princess Taycapin reclined at once inside her portable house of woven *capa* bark, called in the chief of her tirewomen, and ordered that her toilet be arranged ceremonially, as it had not been since the party rode into the jungle many days since.

The princess had come thus far from her accustomed refinements due to a peculiar severity of the Mayan law, one laid down seven generations previously by her ancestor, the founder of the Third Dynasty. He, perceiving that the wild peccary, the Central American pig, was growing scarce, had decreed that this succulent animal, so desired as a fine morsel, should never again be hunted, except by the members of the royal household.

For, even that far back, two hundred years before, it was apparent to the rulers of Maya that food was growing scarce and must be preserved. No food was more relished than the flesh of the wild peccary; and it had been made a crime for any but royalty to eat flesh.

So the Princess Taycapin, wishing to present her brother Za Ramna with peccaries for a feast during the coming sacrifices, had come forth to the hunt.

This was in the Twelfth Century, when the first fecund seeds of the mighty explorations which were to open the unknown lands of the earth had been sown, by the sons of Eric the Red, among the Vikings of the North.

INSIDE THE CAPA tent the toilet of the princess proceeded with as much haste as was compatible with royal formality.

When she was ready to step from under the *capa* roof into the divine glance of the Supreme God Sun, there would be placed across her shoulders the priceless *huitzin*. This would be fastened with a necklace of chalcedony and jade, and would fall back from her shoulders and drag on the ground, like any royal robe—or like the gorgeous tail of a peacock. It was not clothing—it was illustrious and regal decoration—this *huitzin*, softer than any silk ever known, more lustrous in subtle and exquisite coloring than any cloth ever woven by man.

For the *huitzin* was made of the breasts of humming birds, and only the wrens, and these taken only in the superb moment preceding the fulfillment of the mating instinct. Each bird could contribute the material for a piece of fabric no more than quarter of an inch in diameter.

It was not only priceless. For any other than its royal owner to wear it was a crime punishable by death from slow torture which began by opening a space between the lumbar vertebrae and exposing the lungs to the outer air.

Taycapin rose as a shout came from the jungle. It was the

announcement of the approach of her captain. She stood to receive him in the middle of her tent while two women remained a little in the rear, bearing the *huitzin*.

"Enter!" she called, as she lifted her hand, on whose forefinger gleamed the gold signet ring in the form of the leaping jaguar—the symbol of authority.

Not daring to gaze upon her directly, the captain came to the door of the tent and prostrated himself on the ground. This was an awkward and difficult gesture because of his armor, made of quilted cotton an inch thick.

With his nose in the earth the captain exclaimed, "I have seen, O Highness!"

"What have you seen, fool?"

"The Gods on the Waters!"

"Rise, dolt!"

The captain obeyed, while the cotton corselet, because of its cunning jointures, slid over the flexing of his body. Yet he held his eyes down.

"Approach!"

He came a step nearer, trembling. For a soldier to be inside the royal tent was dangerous. A special ceremony was required of persons who entered there, and he, poor common man, knew not what it was. He might at any moment, through ignorance, commit a crime which would be punishable by death.

The stern voice of the princess made him tremble. There was something in her of stone and something of the rattlesnake. Something not feminine—nor yet only royal. The mere tone of her voice filled the soldier with monstrous fear, yet he dared only strive to obey and pray that she would shortly dismiss him.

"YOU HALF-BLIND IDIOT!" began the princess, acridly. The captain felt he was shriveling as he lowered his head. "Search your mind and heart and speak truth. Mind that you speak to Taycapin, daughter of Quexamatl, descendant of the Sun God. Mind that if you utter blasphemy you die!"

"*Aie!*"

"Speak sense, miserable captain. What have you seen?"

"I saw gods, Highness! As I live, as I breathe, as I tremble with joy in the august presence of the daughter of Quexamatl, I have seen but now the faces and forms of the Greater Gods of Maya!"

Still his eyes were averted and with difficulty he restrained his impulse to bolt and run.

"Gods!" The royal lady spoke still sternly, but despite herself a trace of respect came into her strident voice. "A soldier may not see the gods. It is unlawful!"

The captain went to his knees. This was what he had dreaded—he knew that it was a crime for a common man to look upon a god, and yet he had but obeyed the royal order. He bowed his head humbly. It did not once enter his mind to question any decree that might emanate from his queenly mistress.

If she had ordered his heart torn out the next moment, he would neither have been surprised nor would he have offered the least resistance. Now he was unable to speak.

"Rise!" ordered the terrible woman. "Rise and proceed to the water's edge and bring them here!"

He stumbled to his feet. The order filled him with horror. He would have been supine before an order from her lips for his own execution—not before this.

"Pardon, Highness!" he stammered. "Who am I that I may order a god?"

"They are but men. Bring them here."

"Oh, Highness!" He fell prostrate, full length, at her feet, with his nose in the dirt. "Do not ask me to touch the gods! Tear out my heart, dismember my body, but do not ask me to destroy my soul!"

The poignant intensity of fear in her captain gave Princess Taycapin pause. She, too, averted her glance. A trace of fear entered her stern countenance. After a moment she stepped toward the opening in the tent, while she motioned her women to place the *huitzin* over her shoulders.

Then she said solemnly, "I will go."

2

ROREK THE RED

ON THE SANDY shore a vessel was rolling in through the surf, skillfully guided by the world's most audacious sailors. Seven of them; gaunt, raw-ribbed men of huge stature. Six had flaxen hair. The seventh, the youthful leader, taller than any of the others and more slender, with bluer eyes, was particularly conspicuous because of his flaming red hair. A fiery red, brighter far than brick. In the sun it had the quick life of burnished copper.

"Olav!" he cried to the man at the fore gunwale. "Over the side! We touch!"

"Aye, Rorek!"

The foremost leaped into the surf. In the trough of the waves the water reached his shoulders. The next crest engulfed him, but he clung to the gunwale, guiding it in.

"All out!" cried the leader.

"Aye, Rorek!"

Five others followed the first. Only the red-haired chief remained, his hand upon the tiller. The prow of the vessel thus lifted skimmed on swiftly, while the men, wading in the water, three on each side, helped it along.

There ensued a confusion of orders and a swift fury of activity during the perilous moment of beaching the craft.

"Lift her prow, Olav! Give him your hand, Eric!" cried the leader.

In a short time she was safely beached, after which the men propped her in the sands with the huge oars lifted from their thwarts.

Rorek's first thought was to inspect his vessel. He passed all around her, examining her sides. She was made of hand-hewn oak timbers, each about eight inches wide, held with wooden pins, and the seams closed with wolf hair soaked in pitch.

This vessel of Rorek the Red—the Black Hawk they called it—was nearly ninety feet in length and was twenty feet in the beam. Yet it drew no more than three feet of water. As Rorek often said, "it could swim on the dew of a cow pasture or it could cross the Atlantic." He was too modest to add, as he should have added, "if properly manned."

Now, as he examined the seams along her sides, Rorek's eyes lighted with delight. Some of the deep lines in his strong countenance, engraved by hunger and privation, became softened, and a caressing tone crept into his hard voice as he said to his chief oarsman, "Hai, Olav! See the Hawk's wings! Not a feather injured in her long flight!"

Before Olav could reply, a shout from the edge of the near-by reeds brought them all to eager attention. The chief archer, Eric, had been reconnoitering.

"Beware! Beware!" he cried. "I see a man!"

They rushed for protection to the side of the ship, reaching up for their shields which hung over the thwarts. Quickly they placed the shields on left arms, and from pegs behind took long bows and quivers of arrows.

SO INBRED WAS the military spirit, so precise the discipline that within the briefest space of time the seven presented a glancing phalanx to the misty shore and mysterious jungle beyond. Rorek at the head, his red thatch like an oriflamme; the six at regular intervals behind, shields touching each other and fully protecting all vital parts of all bodies, save the faces and necks.

"I see nothing!" said Rorek.

"He is there, behind that clump of trees," insisted Eric.

"It may be only an animal!"

Olav, the third in line, muttered, "Beware! We thought it was only an animal up there—to the north—when we landed."

"Aye!" added Eric, "and it was a nest of savages, and they slew Hjalmar and Wotin. Beware!"

Eric neglected to mention that Hjalmar, one of the sturdiest of the Norse adventurers, had first, without provocation, slain his twain of natives.

Rorek realized full well how that massacre had happened, up there in the savannas, hundreds of miles to the north. Already he had sensed the pacific character of the natives of these far Western shores; realized their childlike curiosity and trust; appreciated that they would strike only when at bay and in fear of their lives. For Rorek had a vision and an insight into the baffled bosom of humanity.

"These be other men—if men they are!" he counseled. "Let us give them no cause for anger!"

"Strike first, is best!" mumbled Eric.

"Aye! Plant in them the fear of Thor's hammer—at once!" protested the emboldened Olav.

Meanwhile the phalanx of seven advanced, slowly,

toward the fringe of verdure and low trees which lined the shore. To timid, fluttering, naive eyes, glancing from behind sheltered nooks in the fronds, this seven-plated burnished shield advancing so firmly and courageously must have seemed, a walking fortress, a battlement alive.

Yet the strangers could detect no movement in the low forest—none more than the gentle ripple of the reeds and grasses under the warm breeze that blew in from the great gulf.

Over the brilliant day which was now dispersing the fogs there hung a sense of brooding mystery—a portent of fateful events about to come into the lives of men.

Suddenly, without warning, the sharp twang of tautened gut sang through the moist air. A long arrow sped over the shoulder of the advancing Rorek. A shrill, piercing shriek from the underbrush told of the surety of its aim.

Rorek glanced back darkly. The rearmost archer, the gloomy-browed, narrow-eyed Wolfkin was reaching for another arrow in his quiver. "How dare you!" cried the chief.

"It's a brown bear! See!" jabbered Wolfkin, pointing excitedly to the forest. All looked ahead, and saw something floundering in the undergrowth.

The phalanx broke, as fear of human opposition dissipated with this announcement. Rorek was the first to reach the spot where the "brown bear" lay impaled.

It was a creature such as those eyes, well accustomed to all the lore of woodcraft, had never seen before. The arrow had pierced its shoulder, which had happened to be a few inches from a sapling, to which it had been impaled. Against the sapling it hung, limp, without a struggle.

Rorek went to it fearlessly, seized the arrow by the shank

and drew it forth. The brown body slumped to the earth, while Rorek looked down upon it with curious amazement.

"This is no bear!" he said; "it is a man!"

HE STOOPED AND lifted the strange form in his stalwart arms. It was that of one of the peccary scouts of the Princess Taycapin, a figure about four feet ten in height, and encased in the cotton armor of the Mayan warrior. The fuzzy surface of this cotton armor, dyed a sepia brown, had fooled Wolfkin.

The arrow had gone through the armor, pinning its wearer to the sapling, but had not broken the flesh. The collapse of the warrior was due to a faint—his apprehension of instant death. As he regained consciousness in the arms of Rorek his eyes opened and he gazed, as if bewitched, on the red hair of the stranger. He strove to speak, but his tongue clove to the roof of his mouth.

Rorek set him down. The Mayan groveled on the earth, burrowing his nose in the dirt, and there poured from him a torrent of duck-like sounds.

The chief turned on his amazed archer. He had long considered what he should do in such a case, for that experience in the north had taught him that it was equally important to maintain discipline within his own ranks, and to announce to the alien hosts of this strange land that he had toward them neither fear nor evil intent.

Rorek took a pace toward Wolfkin until the two were separated by no more than an arm's length. Neither could know that more than the lone Mayan warrior was near; yet, in the woods, and along the sides of the nearby barrancas, many distant eyes took note; saw clearly and reported instantly.

They saw the flaming leader with the hair of burnished copper reach forth with his open hand and fell the dark archer to earth with a single blow on the jaw. They could not know the meaning of the words, but the six Norsemen well knew what Rorek meant as he said gruffly:

"I said give no cause for anger. Obey, Wolfkin!"

From the sandy earth, at his feet, the surly Wolfkin growled, "Aye, Rorek!"

"Then, rise! And hold thy arrows until I give the word!"

"Aye!" Sullenly the reproved archer obeyed.

The five looked on, with neither approval nor disapproval. To them it was a very trifling episode of the discipline that was part of such leadership as Rorek's. They knew that he was physically as he was mentally the master of them all.

However, it was no trifling episode for Maya. Back in the forest, along the edge of the marsh, other scouts were spying. While it was unlawful to look upon divinity yet how could they know it was indeed divinity until—

Ah! "Until!" Until they had seen such deeds as could have source only in a god of Maya.

For had they not seen a Mayan warrior stricken with one shaft of light—dead—then resurrected with one caress from the god, while one of his own lesser gods he felled with a touch and revived with a look?

What proof of power was this? What surety of benign intent! And yet an awe-inspiring symbol of the shielded omnipotence which was indicated by these trifles!

If anything more were needed, the red hair clinched it. Among all the millions of Maya there was not one thatch of red hair—nor another pair of blue eyes. Who else could possess red hair and blue eyes save only a god?

And a white skin—white as milk!

From the clouds, beyond the great waters, from the bosom of the Sun as he rested beyond the pillars of the east, came this red-crowned Son of the Sun, this god visiting Maya!

So the word ran on swift tongues of rumor through the forest, from watcher to watcher, back to the fertile fields, and the towns and villages, and through the passes of the circling mountains, far to the citadel of Emperor Za Ramna himself.

3

STRANGE FEASTINGS

AS WOLFKIN ROSE and took his place at the rear of the line of shields Eric called softly to Rorek, "Beware! More men!"

Rorek glanced into the undergrowth and saw the distant glint of some brilliant plumage through the saplings. At first he wondered if it were not some tropical bird—some huge pheasant majestically coming toward him.

Then he saw more of the strange little men in brown, gnomish dwarfs in this quilted garb, deployed on either side and to the rear, and all advancing slowly. Turning to his men Rorek said, "Remain here—on guard. If I am in danger, attack, but await my signal."

Whereupon he dropped his shield in the sand, deposited on it his bow and quiver of arrows, laid over them his long sword, and advanced toward the forest with his sole weapon, his iron dagger which was concealed in his waist, under the deerskin that draped his torso.

Rorek had resolved on one bold stroke—to meet these strangers unarmed and unafraid. It was the second conquering manifestation of his genius.

At the edge of the clearing the Mayans met the Norse-man. In the forefront of the little people stood Taycapin,

First Princess of the empire. From her shoulders fell the gorgeous *huitzin,* scintillant as with innumerable hummingbirds. Her hair, piled high and surmounted by a comb of jade and carnelian, gave her a stature above that of any of her warriors, but the regnant spirit which blazed from her black eyes indicated even better her true measure.

Yet these daring and ambitious eyes fell, as they gazed for the first time on the blond male approaching. She felt grateful that none of her attendants was level with her, that none could witness that almost imperceptible hesitation.

For the moment the tribal and racial instinct, born of centuries of custom and tradition, ruled her. Was she not in the presence of divinity? According to Mayan belief the Sun God was red-haired, and dwelt in the misty East beyond the great waters. Who else could this be than he?

Yet Taycapin—mature, intelligent, crafty—possessed a mind that lifted her a step beyond the Mayans of her time. Did not these warriors of her entourage and the millions of the valleys beyond look upon her as semidivine? And upon her brother, Za Ramna, the Emperor, as fully divine?

Who was she, Taycapin, to quarrel with this belief— especially when its universal acceptance guaranteed her position and her privileges? So, if she were of divinity herself, why should she veil her eyes before the Sun God?

For a moment these instincts, these thoughts struggled within her. Then nature asserted itself. The woman who was a queen in all but temporal power came uppermost. She looked upon this male with human eyes and saw him superb in his fresh and hardy youth, taller than any man she had ever seen, handsomely proportioned, alert, smiling.

In her right hand she raised her manikin sceptre, an

affair of grotesque lines carved from purple obsidian. It was a gesture of formal greeting.

"Hail, O Ra-Mu!" she said. The name she used was the mythical one employed by her people to designate the legendary founder of the race. Her words could have conveyed no greater homage.

To Rorek the syllables meant no more than the quack of a duck. But he recognized the reverential tone. He bowed his head with regal dignity, lifted up his hand, and said, "*Skoal!*"

It was the Norse greeting to the gods, later corrupted to a drinking toast.

So they came within a few paces of each other. At a gesture from her, Taycapin's retainers waited while she advanced, and Rorek's archers kneeled far back on the sands, behind their barricade of shields. For some time they tried their words on each other.

Taycapin began, "O Ra-Mu, swift as the *quetzal,* the plumed eagle; powerful as the jaguar, wise as the serpent, cunning as the ape, all-seeing as the Sun, thrice welcome are you to the miserable shores of Maya!"

NOT COMPREHENDING A word, Rorek replied in his mighty voice: "We have had nothing to drink for twenty days except the rainwater we could soak from our sailcloth. Our food is nearly gone. But we are strong. My men can kill anything that runs or flies or swims, but I have bade them to hold back their arrows. We come as friends!"

Taycapin recognized this as the language of divinity because she could not understand it. She replied, "O Ra-Mu! We worship you. My brother, Za Ramna, wretched worm that he is, unworthy descendant of our common ancestor, will welcome you at Uxmal if you will but come!"

For reply Rorek placed his hand on his stomach and opened his mouth to indicate the great cavity within. This eloquence was comprehended by the princess. With that comprehension came a tiny rift in her confidence in the origin of the stranger. He was hungry, but should a god be hungry?

It was a question to be stowed away in the recesses of her mind to be brought forth later, and to be pondered over. For the present she responded with equal eloquence by clapping her hands, whereupon the nearest warrior came forward, head averted so he would not profane divinity with his mundane glance, and received an order from his mistress.

He scuttled back into the forest and presently returned with an armful of coconuts. One of his fellows assisted him in breaking one, which was handed to Taycapin. After she had blessed it by passing over it the obsidian manikin, she offered it to Rorek.

He looked at the coconut blankly. It was the first he had ever seen. The princess showed him what to do by drinking some of the milk.

When Rorek tasted the cool freshness of the milk of the coconut he visibly expanded. If he was a god here was nectar. If he was divinity here was ambrosia.

He would stand no longer on ceremony. He waved to his archers to approach. They had been hungrily and thirstily observing. They threw down their shields and their bows, their arrows and their swords and rushed for the heap of coconuts which had by now been piled before the princess.

The coconuts, with their delicious milk, proved to be only a cocktail for the feast the Princess Taycapin spread before her Norse guests. Mutual confidence having been established she led the way back to her *capa* tent.

At once she decided, without reference to the High Priest, Pocapa Tlal, august interpreter of the laws of Maya, that the peccaries she had secured for the table of her brother, should be offered to him she hailed as Ra-Mu. It was a momentous act.

While the peccaries were steaming in a pit, rush baskets were passed among the guests. First came a pudding of maize and squash; then one of yams. Another was piled high with chirimoya, a soft, aromatic fruit. Another combined a collection of avocados, or alligator pears. There were also papayas, guavas and custard apples, and cashew nuts and peanuts.

LONG BEFORE THE peccaries were ready, the hungry archers were stuffed, but then gourds were passed which amazingly revived their failing appetites. These contained a thick sweetish liquor, distilled from the cactus plant, highly alcoholic.

As the fiery shafts of the *mishla* aroused them, Eric and Olav seized Wolfkin and the others and danced with them about the pit where the steam from the stewing pigs was dying down. It was a weird, gaunt shuffle, thrusting the knees out and up, throwing the arms above the head, shouting, and carrying through all a fierce chant of thanksgiving. A Druid paean to the god of feasts. The Norse expression of Bacchic fury.

Although Rorek ate, he remained aloof and dignified. He had barely tasted the *mishla,* recognized its fiery tang for that of alcohol, and realized that some one must remain sober. Moreover, he observed that the Princess Taycapin did not drink the fiery stuff.

It was no time to be drunk. Here were strange peoples; new adventures; a civilization of which he and his had never even dreamed. If this was but the fringe, what was the garment like?

He would need all his wit to meet what this strange land might bring.

4

A BOLD PLAN

THE NEXT DAY the Princess Taycapin realized that she had committed what might turn out to be a blasphemous crime. Certainly it was an indiscretion. She had fed the peccaries that were the Emperor's to this attractive stranger; and if he should prove to be no god—

Rorek was expert in learning new tongues. In his way that great traveler was a linguist. The first day he knew a dozen Mayan words; the next day a score. Promptly he learned, from words and looks, that the store of Mayan meat was depleted, though he was yet to learn the religious significance of peccary meat. So he offered to replete the larder.

However, the peccaries proved both scarce and elusive. The hunt led the cotton soldiers and the Norse archers through the jungle day after day, for weeks.

The princess did not mind. She was teaching a willing pupil the words and the ways of Maya.

One morning Rorek assembled his archers about him. "We have replaced the animals that we have eaten," he announced, "and to-day we start inland."

Eric involuntarily exclaimed, "if we leave the vicinity of our stout vessel, O Chief, we are lost!"

"We are guests. We will go where we are taken."

When this was communicated to the others, they gathered about Rorek in frightened protest. The idea of going away, of leaving their vessel, of following inland a gaudy stranger who knew how to cook spicy meats and brew crazing drinks was abhorrent to their simple Norse minds.

For generations they and theirs had been descending on strange coasts, but in such an event the procedure never varied. Enter the nearest settlement by force of arms, loot its treasure, seize its strong men who remained alive, enjoy its women and then abandon them and repair to the boats and escape before succor could arrive. That was the immemorial Norse custom. For on their boats—swift, predatory, the speediest racing craft known—they relied as relied the Romans on their short swords.

Now Galko and Hemnet, Olav and Eric Wolfkin and Donal exercised the privilege of freeborn Norsemen to question the decision of a leader at the crisis of an expedition. Vehemently they counseled the age-honored way.

"We have obeyed, Rorek, son of the great king," said Galko. "We are yours on the sea, in storm or calm; yours to command. Yours in battle to use as you see fit! Yours on the march, without fear or question. But, O Chief, now that we have survived the perils of the deep, now that we have buried our fallen comrades and have come upon the promised land, rich with slaves and wine and precious stones, we claim our toll! Give the word! Unleash us! There be women here—we would have them! There be riches—we would seize them! Unhand us, O Chief!"

"Aye!" raucously added the bovine Olav, "that head woman wears green stones that sparkle—many of them.

My uncle knew a Saxon who bartered with a Frank for a green stone like that—only a fraction of the size—which the Frank had from a Phoenician galley out of Alexandria; and it passed with the king for a ransom for his life. Green stones are very rare. That woman has many. I may seize and take the stones."

"Aye!" muttered Hemnet. "Did you see that robe she wears—of every color, and none? The color changes as she walks. I'll wager a witch concocted it by moonlight. It is worth seizing."

"Ya!" Wolfkin sneered. "Take your stones and your robe, and the gold, too, which I saw on the wrists and neck of the woman, but give me that one who lit the torch at the feast. She is small and thin, but I want her. Give her me, O Chief!"

ROREK LISTENED GRAVELY and silently. He realized they felt prompted by a Norse sense of justice. He waited for them to sputter out their protest to the full, waited until no one had more to say, waited until they all hung stolidly on his words. Finally he spoke in the low voice which became him. Strange that he, youngest of all, should yet be the leader.

"Men," he said simply, "what you claim is by right yours!"

"Hai!" shouted the impetuous Wolfkin, starting to dart off toward the hidden tent in the forest where he had last seen the princess's slender tirewoman.

"Yet I ask you to listen!" Rorek calmly went on. Wolfkin and the others listened. "We are very far from home—more than six seasons. The storms have blown us from our course again and again. We do not know how we may return—or when. Is it not so?"

"Aye!" came the wondering chorus. He waited respect-fully until each one could assent.

"Now, for the second time we come upon natives who are kind to us. These are not like the Saxons or the Franks or the Normans. Nor are they like those natives we met to the north. These are friendly people. If we abuse them, if we attack without good cause, we have only placed enemies in our path.

"But if we return kindness with kindness, they will welcome us even as have those who spread the feast last night, and we will find a new home—far from home."

The six looked at one another blankly. This was queer talk. Far beyond their logical processes. Was Rorek a bit mad? Had the strain of the adventure cracked his wit?

Presently he talked a little more rationally. "Men," he went on, impetuously, "I will tell you more. Inland from here dwell the people from whom these came—a great people—rich. They have heaps of green stones; great vaults of yellow gold; storehouses filled with good food and colored raiment. And I, your Chief, Rorek, son of the King Ha-Aton, counsel you to withhold your hands. We will go on. We will go on to the great cities of this people. There we will find many women and great riches."

"How do you know this?" demanded Wolfkin, a bit impudently.

"From her!" Rorek gestured toward the tent of Taycapin.

"How can you talk with her without knowing her language?"

"She has told me!" The blond giant drew himself to his full height of six feet three. "The princess has told Rorek, son of King Ha-Aton!"

The tone was enough, the rebuke sufficient, for Wolfkin and the others. They nodded assent. Yet Olav stolidly voiced the fear that seemed prevalent among them, as he objected, "But, O Chief, if there are so many, how dare we trust ourselves among them? Why not capture these few first? There are no more than a hundred. They are so small and worthless that it will be easy."

"If we harm these it will arouse the others."

"If we take these it will place in the others the fear of Thor's hammer!" Gaiko cried.

"Peace!" Rorek commanded. "These people believe we are gods. The gods do not conquer by fear. They are gods!"

Rorek's red oriflamme rose proudly.

"Thor is a god," Wolfkin grumbled, "and his hammer puts the fear of the gods in every one!"

"Hold thy tongue, Wolfkin!" Rorek harshly added, as he saw the Princess Taycapin come from her tent. "We are not the gods of the storm and the lightning. We are the Gods of the Sun!"

He bowed graciously as the little woman approached and held out his hand, palm upward.

5

THE DEVIL AND THE HIGH PRIEST

WITHIN THE HOUR they began the march into the jungle. It was slow going, along paths made by beasts—the ocelot, the jaguar, the peccary, the tapir.

The afternoon of the second day Rorek shot a *trogon*—the famous and rare Central American *quetzal,* bearing brilliant copper-colored tail feathers—a bird sacred to the Mayans.

At first Taycapin was horror-stricken. If this were known, what would the High Priest say? Then, as with an inspiration, she greeted him with, "O Quetzalcoatl!"

It was a combining of the words meaning sacred plumage and serpent. The name was to cling to him always. "The Plumed Serpent." The repository of all earthly wisdom, lit by the brilliance of the skies.

A few days later they entered the cultivated lands and passed through maize fields and long windrows of growing vegetables. The Norsemen could not but be impressed with the evidence of industry and skill. Then came houses, often well built, of limestone and stucco, colored variously with inlaid shell and applied pigment.

Though these people were of puny physique, their

achievements revealed great industry and an organizing brain at their head.

Thus, possibly, the Goths under Alaric felt as they crowded in on the Roman forum from their barbaric northern camps.

Yet ominous signs attended them. Chiefly an ever-recurrent not unmusical sound on a conch shell, whose wielder was seldom seen. The signal echoed and reechoed along the way as they proceeded.

It was the Mayan conch-shell telegraph carrying news of their approach ahead of them.

They saw people—but only in the distance, and running away.

The dour Donal complained to Rorek. "The air is not healthy."

"Aye," added Eric, "they are preparing an ambush!"

Beware!" groaned Wolfkin.

Rorek quieted them, but went to Taycapin.

"Do not fear," said the princess, "we approach Mayapan, home of the High Priest, Pocapa Tlal. There all will be well!"

"Fear?" Rorek's laugh boomed out. He would die with a laugh like that.

In a little while, nestling in the hills beyond, at the base of a mountain, they saw the roofs and towers of a city, rising out of the cultivated fields.

"Mayapan!" they heard the cotton soldiers say to one another. Taycapin had explained to Rorek that this was the five-century-old home of the head of Maya's religious order.

As a cloud of dust appeared out of the far horizon, Rorek

called a sharp word of command to Eric. Eric spoke to the others. In a brief moment the six archers assembled, two abreast, their shields held above their heads, and locked, each to the other, with the overlapping snap used to clasp them to the thwarts of the ship.

Thus, six feet in air, was formed a solid flooring of interlocked shields—the buckler throne of the Norse viking. For centuries in the forests and along the fjords of the North, ascension of the buckler throne meant the coronation of a chief. Thus his men proclaimed to the world that here was their acknowledged strongest.

Now, out of the cloud of dust, appeared, on the trot, a file of soldiers—coming toward Taycapin and her guest.

Just as the newcomers drew near enough for the Norsemen to distinguish their figures, Rorek, with a shout, leaped lightly, shield on arm, sword in hand, to the spliced tops of the leveled shields of his archers. Simultaneously the archers split the air with a mighty shout of triumph, announcing to all the world that here, and here alone, dwelt the person of the king.

THE COTTON SOLDIERS stopped, panic-stricken at this sudden apparition of a walking fortress, on whose stout walls stood the omnipotent creature who dared eat peccary and slay a *quetzal*.

But the warriors coming on, at a trot, were more vigorous and less emotional men.

Swarthy, with black beards, each was clothed in a puma skin, a rich tawny yellow. Each carried in one hand a stone-tipped lance and on his side wore a quiver of arrows and a bow.

Taycapin and her escort came to a sharp halt. Rorek

on his buckler throne halted. The advancing puma skins swept down upon them on the double-quick. It seemed for a moment as if they would attack and Olav, from below, grumbled that the Norse archers should nave a chance to get to their weapons and not be compelled to stand on stupidly as buckle bearers.

Rorek stood with superb ease, resting on his shield, atop the throne.

The puma-clad warriors broke when they reached the princess, flowed on each side and beyond the Norsemen. It was clear that their officers, had told them not to look at the strangers, but a few dared steal a glance. This Rorek noted. His hawk-like eyes missed nothing.

There must have been several thousand of the puma-clad ones. Soon they completely filled the road and surged over into the fields, both front and rear of the princess and Rorek.

Then, in the wake, appeared a gorgeous litter, twice the size of the elegant one which bore the princess. It came to a halt directly before her and from it stepped a squat figure of a man. He was obese, with broad shoulders, heavy paunch, and a beak of a nose, with piercing eyes and pouchy jowls.

A gorgeous *huipila,* or Mayan skirt, embroidered in gold and emeralds, clothed his thighs, while he was nude from the waist up, except for the row on row of jade, chalcedony and carnelian ornaments which clanked on his breast and back.

On his appearance the puma-clad army bowed, as one man.

"Pocapa Tlal!" came in a dim murmur, "Mighty one!"

He advanced to the princess, scowling. Rorek could not

hear clearly what was said, but he knew the princess was on the defensive.

In a moment Pocapa Tlal waddled down the road toward Rorek, who, from his twelve-foot height looked curiously down upon him.

The Norseman realized full well that here was a crisis. The next few minutes might easily decide his fate—death, if he made a mistake. Should he retain his advantage of height and distance on the buckler throne, or should he voluntarily relinquish it?

When Pocapa Tlal was within twenty feet the priest stopped, and stoutly gazed at the strange spectacle of six giants holding on their shields a seventh—and he red-haired.

The High Priest had just one flicker of hesitation, one brief moment of doubt, as he spread his legs firmly to reassure himself that he had solid earth beneath his feet.

Rorek did not miss the flicker of hesitation. With a gay shout he leaped to the earth and advanced to meet the High Priest. He left his shield and sword, and bow and arrow behind.

A look of crafty triumph passed over the face of Pocapa Tlal. He raised his right hand aloft. In it was the black obsidian *pecate*, an object fifteen inches long, carved in the figure of a jaguar with the tail of a rattlesnake—symbol of divine authority. When he waved that all Maya must obey.

The puma soldiers came to quick attention, their right hands at the quivers on their hips, their left hands poising the lances. The Norsemen might have accounted for a score, two score, a hundred of them—but the thousands would have worn them down.

POCAPA TLAL WAS speaking. "Devil!" he addressed Rorek, in a voice so loud all could hear. His warriors drank in his august words. "Devil, who has taken the form of a god to bewilder men, how dare you invade this peaceful land to the very gates of Mayapan!"

"No, O Priest!" Rorek replied. He had learned the Mayan words for this speech from Taycapin, one by one. "I am not a devil. I come in friendship to Maya, from beyond the seas—from the East!"

Pocapa Tlal's mouth fell open. To be addressed in Mayan, so clearly, was something he had not anticipated. For a moment he was checkmated, and then his fear and his dark purpose ruled him. Well he realized that if this stranger were accepted as divine in Maya it might spell the beginning of the end for him and his power.

He lifted higher the black *pecate*, with its grinning jaguar tusk and its swinging rattlesnake tail, and advanced on Rorek. Perhaps he felt a little doubt in his own mind as to the origin of this stranger. Could he be divine?

If he were human he could never withstand the menace of the *pecate*. Pocapa Tlal lifted the symbolic stone.

Instantly, through all the ranks of the puma-clad soldiers ran a swift and galvanic thought without words. Every eye dwelt on that black *pecate*, as every member of an orchestra would dwell on the baton of the leader.

The falling of that *pecate* was a signal never ignored by the puma soldiers. When it struck they struck. Hands gripped lances more firmly. Thousands of feet were braced more tightly on the ground.

Eric, the shrewd and watchful lieutenant, spat out a warning:

"Beware, Chief!"

Wolfkin grumbled to Olav, "See—they are ready to strike!"

"We are lost!" Galko mumbled to Donal.

"I can spit five with one arrow!" Donal glumly replied.

Rorek was never more calm. All five senses—and a sixth—were attuned. He heard the muttered words of his archers; saw the swift gleam of wicked hate in the baleful eyes of the menacing Mayan; he felt the rapid and galvanic assembling in the puma army of the will to attack.

But his purpose in his own mind was clear. If he was to conquer this people it must be by wits. Six archers against as many millions could never win. And he knew the meaning of that *pecate,* for Taycapin had been careful to instruct him.

Under his breath, softly, to Eric, he said, "Hold! On peril of your lives make no move."

Now the voice of Pocapa Tlal shrilled forth in a sing-song, chanting bellow, evidently the chant of a ritual. He was reciting something prepared of old for such occasions.

"Great Ah Puch!" he cried, as he called on the Lord of Death, "deliver the Children of the Sun from this accursed peril to their homes and fields. Lift up thy arm, Ah Puch; lift up thy strong right arm—"

The *pecate* trembled in mid-air. It rose even to the level of the eyes of the Norseman, and there paused while Pocapa Tlal, wheezy with his unwonted emotion, went deep for a final breath with which to launch the lethal curse.

In that second Rorek struck—swiftly and surely as the paw of a jaguar from behind a dark tree on a moonlit road in the jungle.

From his waist appeared swiftly his iron dagger. With a single movement he brought it down smartly across the tusk of the stone jaguar, and the *pecate* fell in the dust of the road, shattered.

Pocapa Tlal stuttered, stopped, fell back a step. The sweat broke forth on his brow.

The Norsemen could feel the tension break in the puma army; could see the clenched hands on the stone-tipped lances relax and tremble; could hear the muttered gasps of awe and wonderment.

Among superstitious people to whom symbols meant everything, this conspicuous and vivid exhibition was decisive.

Rorek sheathed his dagger, smiled, leaned down and picked up from the dust of the road the severed pieces of the obsidian *pecate*.

Then, with a regal gesture, and a lordly smile, utterly composed, he held them forth in the open palm to the High Priest.

6

DOOMED

"ON! TO UXMAL—AND the Emperor!"

Rorek had resumed his exalted place on the buckler throne. His left arm bore the long elliptical shield, which covered him from throat to knees, but was held carelessly forward on a jaunty angle, as if flaunting a decoration that would be warlike only on compulsion. His right hand thrust aloft and ahead his long sword, whose tip was a full fifteen feet from the dusty red clay of the Mayan road.

A truly imposing figure. Regal! Divine! At least it seemed so to those thousands who witnessed it that soft warm day in early spring.

The puma soldiers, who had witnessed the unprecedented, the audacious shattering of the *pecate*, tried to keep their eyes on Pocapa Tlal, yet ever they shifted their gaze to the inspiring Norseman with his shining sword and his flaming red hair.

Pocapa Tlal looked at the obsidian symbol. The rattlesnake had been broken from the jaguar. Though it was his business to employ superstition to his own ends and to use its power over the populace, rather than to be used by it, now the force he dealt in turned to rend him.

He became a victim, temporarily, of the superstitious fear

that if he persisted in opposition to the stranger, openly, at least, this broken symbol might flower into actuality. If his physical force, typified by the jaguar, was to be separated from his divine wisdom, typified by the rattlesnake, what would become of Pocapa Tlal?

The High Priest decided on discretion—for the moment. To give himself a little more breathing space. To study this arrogant stranger. He did not believe Rorek was a god, but what was he? Never before had anyone in Maya seen such a man.

As a matter of fact Pocapa Tlal was not at all sure what his gods actually did look like. Though he was professionally in the god business, and owed his enormous power over vast multitudes to his supposed intimacy with the gods, he had never seen one. Nor had he ever pretended to see one.

Like all other Mayan priests he always represented the gods hazily. When his artists represented them in carvings they showed only portions of heads and then let the bodies slope off into the mist of nothingness.

Pocapa Tlal, in the mere routine of his duties, was continually bringing messages to the people from the Sky God, who looked something like a cloud, and from the Maize God who seemed to be a good-looking youth until he flowered into an ear of corn, and from the Death God Ah Puch who looked like a bag of bones—and who had just betrayed him; from the Long-nosed God of Rain who had no body below his weeping eyes, and from the Rainbow God who had neither head nor tail.

The High Priest had never demeaned himself to the point of actually saying he had seen these gods. Was it not enough for the groveling sons and daughters of Maya that he brought them authentic messages?

Now he was not a little curious, and not a little disturbed. In the Mayan mythology there was Ah Puch, the Lord of Death, and Ra-Mu, the Lord of Life. Taycapin had sent word that this stranger was Ra-Mu. Nonsense. Ra-Mu was the legendary founder of the race, riding on a cloud of the east thousands of years before. And always the Lord of Life—most potent force in Mayan thought.

Yet, if the people should believe he was Ra-Mu? There lay danger.

It was not until later that Pocapa Tlal learned Taycapin had named the stranger Quetzalcoatl. The Plumed Serpent! That was even more insidious, because it was more plausible than that he was the Lord of Life. As a Plumed Serpent he would combine heavenly and wordly wisdom. He would not only be a rival, he must inevitably supersede Pocapa Tlal himself, who was merely a High Priest, and had been one for only ten years.

UNDER HIS SCOWLING black brows these malevolent reflections went on silently. Outwardly Pocapa Tlal diplomatically stepped aside for the princess and this stranger.

He stood in the dust, the broken *pecate* in his hand, while the buckler throne went on. He almost forgot the serried might of his puma-clad army until his chief captain stepped up and asked for instructions.

"Fall in!" he said, gruffly. "Compose a guard of honor!"

He himself was surprised at the order. He had come forth from Mayapan fully determined to destroy this stranger before he reached the gates of the city; yet here he was, following humbly in his wake as he proceeded on.

With one stout gesture Rorek had thus averted the sheathed lightning. Was this godlike or not? Pocapa Tlal himself wondered.

Ahead Rorek did not wait for the princess. He realized full well the significance of what he had done, and the importance of his triumph. He hastened on now to consolidate it.

As he came abreast the princess cried, from her litter, "Less haste, O Quetzalcoatl! Permit me to proceed and show the way!"

"My men do not stop, Princess. Do you follow on!"

So the procession entered Mayapan, Rorek heading it gloriously on his buckler throne, the princess coming next with her escort of cotton-armored warriors, to be followed in turn by the litter of Pocapa Tlal and his swart army.

Mayapan was a city with a quarter of a million people. They lived in long rectangular streets of houses, two and even three stories high, made of dried mud, often covered with stucco. As many as fifteen lived in a single room.

The inhabitants poured out like ants from an aroused hill. For two days they had known of the approach of this extraordinary stranger. First the rumor had spread that the Princess Taycapin had said he was a god; that was shortly set at rest from the steps of the temple by the herald of Pocapa Tlal himself who had announced the stranger was no more than a devil pretending he was a god; he added that all good Mayapan folk should rest secure, for the High Priest would go forth with his dread puma army and exorcise the devil before he could do any damage.

Yet here came the devil himself. Or was he a god? Riding

buoyantly on the head of giants, a red foam of divinity on his head, the seal of the lightning in his hand!

A seething activity preceded and followed him on his way through the streets, as he pressed on toward the colored temple he could see at the base of a prominence in the center. Most of the population, timid, utterly subservient to Pocapa Tlal, hid themselves in their houses. But many thousands peered out timorously, from corners, from windows, balconies, alleys as the buckler throne passed.

Before the temple Rorek halted. This was only because he was not sure of the road beyond. When Taycapin arrived he called down to the litter, without deigning to get down from his eminence:

"Which way to Uxmal, O Princess?"

"That way!" she said, pointing. "But we stop here this night, as guests of Pocapa Tlal."

"No!" cried Rorek. "I prefer your brother!"

With that the buckler throne was off. Taycapin was too bewildered to do else than follow. As soon as they were clear of the city Rorek leaped to the ground and walked with his archers, that they might rest for their next imposing but exacting performance.

"Look!" Eric said loudly, some time later.

They stared ahead toward Uxmal, and saw two people approaching.

FAR IN ADVANCE marched one, a queer little figure, even smaller than the other Mayans they had seen. His purple-bound *huipila* indicated that he was of the royal household.

"Ah!" said Rorek. "Perhaps Za Ramna is coming to greet us."

In a few minutes Taycapin came up and got out of her

litter. At sight of her the little man increased his pace, and in a moment came near enough to be heard, as he called, "Greetings, O wife!"

Rorek was not entirely sure of the word, though his lingual talent and his close attention to Taycapin's instructions in the language had made him already fairly adept in Mayan.

He repeated the word wonderingly. "Wife?"

Taycapin seemed annoyed.

"He is just one of my husbands!" she said.

To conceal his astonishment Rorek translated this for the benefit of the archers. They were immediately convulsed in merriment.

"One!" grunted Donal. "He looks like a small half portion."

Rorek turned back to the princess. "How many husbands have you?" he asked.

"Only four."

"Only four!"

Rorek could not conceal his surprise. He must have looked blank indeed, for he stepped back a bit and took a deep breath. He had no romantic feeling for her, but it had never occurred to him that Taycapin was else than a maiden.

Evidently she thought his backward step one of balked desire, or frustrated ambition, for at once she went to him and in the simplest and most direct way, without the least concern for the wretched male object in the purple-lined *huipila*, said:

"That need not concern you, O Quetzalcoatl. I married

them before I saw you. I shall send them to the sacrificial stone at the next harvest."

The weary little male turned waxy pale and his knees shook, but he uttered not a sound.

Rorek opened his mouth to protest, but Taycapin went on calmly, and almost casually, "I shall marry you, Quetzalcoatl, and have but one husband; that is best."

The Norseman flushed a fiery red. For a moment his skin almost matched his hair, and while the intense little princess clung on his words for an affirmative, he was spared the dread necessity of committing himself just then by the approach of the second figure.

Rorek looked up to behold the fairest sight he had ever seen. It was a maiden astride a llama. A maiden perhaps sixteen or seventeen years old. Skin of a light olive texture. Eyes of lustrous brown. Wavy black hair, hanging to her waist. Devoid of ornament as of clothing, save only one piece.

That was the priceless *huitzin*, which hung, not from her shoulders, but flowing about her middle—suggesting the soft throb of humming birds in the afternoon air.

It was the garment of royalty, but not worn with authority. It was worn as the ancients wore sackcloth, in mourning for something departed.

The lonely figure on the llama turned on the crossroad, branching off toward Chichen Itza.

"Who is she?" asked Rorek.

"The annual sacrifice."

Rorek felt his heart constrict as if he had been hit a terrific blow.

"Sacrifice?" he cried. "That innocent maid? Sacrifice for what?"

"That the crops may be fruitful for Maya. One life that a hundred million may be spared."

"Who is she?"

"The Chief Virgin of the Sun."

"But why does she wear the garment of royalty?"

"She is the daughter of Za Ramna."

"Daughter of the Emperor?"

"The same."

"By Thor's hammer! What an outrage! That lovely creature!" Rorek felt his breast would explode and burst his armor. He started impetuously toward the disappearing slender figure on the gracefully undulating llama.

The princess seized him with a tenacious grip and clung to him desperately while she adjured:

"Beware, O Quetzalcoatl! One who would so much as speak to the Sun Virgin would be destroyed at once. All the millions of Maya would rise in wrath to curse and rend him!"

7

ROYAL DIPLOMACY

AS THEY NEARED Uxmal, Princess Taycapin stopped her litter to change bearers. Rorek left his archers for the moment and approached.

"What is the name of your brother's daughter?" he asked.

"What is that?" testily replied the princess.

"The name of the fair one we saw just now—the lovely virgin on the strange beast—her name, O Princess?"

"Oh! Her name is Za Chel."

"Za Chel!" Rorek sighed.

Taycapin cast a sharp glance at him; and the march was resumed.

The swift tropic night had now fallen, and still they were passing among the fields of maize and pumpkins and squash and yams, which stretched interminably along the road.

Slaves bore torches made of a bituminous black gum taken from the earth near a limestone quarry far away. They burned evenly in the still air, and seemed like gentle stars come to earth for man's guidance.

Rorek welcomed the dark. He was not obliged to study the country through which he was passing, hostile though it might be. Instead, he could think of that name—Za Chel—and the figure who bore it.

Za Chel. That meant rainbow. So Taycapin had told him in one of those eager lessons of his first days in Maya.

Rainbow! The color that came from the sun out of a wet moon. That came from nowhere, passed through everything, and went no one knew where. The all-suffusing warmth, variety and incident of life and living!

It was pleasant to think about. He was oblivious of the myriad dusky eyes peering at him from the obscure shadows as he passed; oblivious of any danger; oblivious of the unfolding wonders of his advance into the inner fastness of this curious, new people.

Za Chel!

AT UXMAL, IN his red palace, Emperor Za Ramna awaited the approach of his sister and the disquieting stranger.

He had ordered that his soldiers—the jaguar soldiers— should line the city streets and the plaza before the palace to receive the stranger. These soldiers of his wore jaguar skins to distinguish them from the puma-clad soldiers of Pocapa Tlal. They were more formidable fighters than the puma soldiers.

Za Ramna had issued strict instructions that no untoward demonstration should occur. Meanwhile, he considered just how he should receive this newcomer. There was no precedent to go by, and a ruler must think when he has no precedent.

So Za Ramna puzzled his brain.

As emperor it was his business to talk with the gods on special occasions which were too important for Pocapa

"Kill him with this!" the princess tempted.

Tlal to manipulate, but he had never talked with a god in front of his army, or in view of his people.

Za Ramna did his conversing with gods alone, in secret places, in the inner shrine of the temple, and in the dark. And what they said or looked like was never quite clear, which left his interpretation of what they said largely to his own good judgment to pass on to his loyal subjects, which was as it should be.

Here was a god in the open road, in the sunlight, plainly visible to many thousands gathered back along the plateaus of the fertile valleys awaiting anxiously the outcome of the appearance of this phenomenon.

Za Ramna was indeed puzzled. As an emperor he enjoyed his executive power; the details and difficulties he left to others. He preferred to sit still and pass on things— mostly pass.

For many days he had been thinking of those peccaries Taycapin had spent weeks in hunting, in the marsh on the edge of the far jungle near the sea. Now she had brought him this problem to spoil the peccaries' flavor. Dear! Dear! Just like Taycapin. A tomboy! She had plagued him from birth. Za Ramna was in his fifties. The fires of life were burning low in him. He was not a warlike man, and had never been obliged to deal with sudden danger. This was the most astounding event which had occurred in his lifetime.

He knew already of Rorek's meeting with Pocapa Tlal, of the breaking of the *pecate*, of the further advance through the valleys. He had had advance secret information from Taycapin, in which she had urged him to prepare to receive the great Sun God.

It was something so astounding he could not yet credit it.

For he knew his sister, Taycapin, knew her well; and he never had known her to do or say anything without an object. If she wanted the incredible stranger received as the Sun God there was something in it for Taycapin. What?

As for the discomfiture of Pocapa Tlal, Za Ramna had rather enjoyed that episode as relayed to him by the conch shell telegraph. It was well enough for the too-ambitious High Priest to have a little of his self-esteem dampened.

And yet there was menace in the shattering of that *pecate*. Indeed there was much profoundly disturbing in this oncoming stranger.

That day had given him other cause for deep thought. Za Chel, his favorite daughter, had gone to Chichen Itza to implore the Long-nosed God of Rain, Ah Bolan Dzacab, to send his favors to Maya.

Za Chel, the fairest of all his daughters, the only one who as a babe had slept by his side—after her mother died in childbirth. Za Chel! It was almost inevitable that she should go to the Dread Well. If not this season—then another. So went, sooner or later, every Chief Virgin of the Sun.

WHILE THE EMPEROR in his palace was trying to decide how he should receive the mysterious stranger, Rorek himself, in the dust of the long road, was deciding how he should approach the emperor.

The buckler throne had done its part with the high priest and the populace. He might not have a chance to use its unique display with the ruler of the people.

As for being a god, or pretending to be one, he knew very well he would not be likely to impose on Za Ramna. Even his sister had seen through that. It might be useful if the Mayans in general believed in his divinity, but the rulers were different.

So he decided to meet Za Ramna on his own ground; simply, frankly, as one great king to another.

So it was when the rams' horns in the plaza at Uxmal sounded their trumpet calls. The tiger soldiers came to attention. Down through the lines of pitch torches came the litter of the Princess Taycapin, and then came Rorek on his buckler throne.

Taycapin alighted at the steps of the palace and signaled to Rorek. He leaped to the earth and went with her, side by side, up the long steps.

The orange and vermilion scarfs at the palace door

parted, and Taycapin and Rorek entered. There sat a man almost square, so wide were his shoulders, so squat his figure, so generous his girth. A jolly, bright-eyed emperor, who lived well and loved all living. A benevolent despot.

Across his shoulders hung negligently the royal *huitzin*. His *huipila* skirt, quite short, coming above his knees, and reaching hardly to the middle of his round stomach, was of exquisite hemp, saffron-colored. On his forehead, suspended by a gold thread, lay the great emerald of Cochibar, a square-cut stone large as the egg of a pigeon. The light from a brazier of burning charcoal reached out and filled the gem with fire.

Rorek, accustomed to rough fabrics and articles of homely use, could only marvel at the rare splendor of these ornaments. They were simple—but of imperial quality.

The emperor folded his arms sedately and bowed ever so slightly. "Welcome, O Friend of Maya!" he said, measuring his words with rare discretion.

Rorek, without weapons, save only his hidden dagger, returned the bow, with an exact measurement of the angle of inclination of the head, and replied, in his best Mayan: "I bring greetings, O Za Ramna, from my father, the Great King, who dwells across the Eastern sea!"

ZA RAMNA HAD given Rorek his opening by calling him "friend of Maya," and he had stepped in cleverly with that ambiguous reference to the far distant kingship beyond the ocean. Well, it was strictly true. Let the emperor and his Mayans make their own interpretation.

Every word being said there in the palace by the ruler and the stranger, whom all must now consider royal, if not indeed divine, was instantly relayed through a thousand to a million tongues, and so spread rapidly back into the valleys and hills and among the far cities.

"It is our pleasure that you become our guest," said Za Ramna.

"We thank you in the name of our father and in our own name," Rorek replied.

The ice seemed broken. All was well. Taycapin said her adieux and Rorek was alone with Za Ramna, who courteously inquired about his archers and gave orders they should be well fed and housed in the rear of the palace.

Then food and drink were placed before the stranger and his host.

Perhaps it would have been more seemly if Rorek had permitted the questions to come first from the emperor, but—he was no more than twenty-five.

Rorek's chief concern, strangely enough, was over that ravishing vision of a lonely girl. Finally he blurted out: "Taycapin told me that was your daughter I saw on yonder road."

Za Ramna was indeed taken aback. What the devil had Taycapin been thinking of? Had she coughed up the innermost secrets of the palace? And here this stranger was referring to her without a title? Yet this stranger did bold things—that none but a king or a god would dare.

"It was," Za Ramna admitted.

"Was she going to the sacrifice?"

"Nay—to the well."

Rorek was still to learn what was the Dread Well of Chichen Itza, with its hideous depths which hid the decayed bones of the fairest daughters of Maya. Still, he was not satisfied. He had a premonition, for there was a hideous episode in his own past which would never be forgotten—never!

"Is she to be sacrificed?" he insisted.

Za Ramna's head went back stoutly. Here was impertinence, unless the stranger were indeed a god. Yet he answered, calmly: "No. She is to make our royal obeisance to the well—for the spring rains, that Maya may prosper."

Rorek's heart leaped. "And does she return to Uxmal?"

"Aye, in the month of Mol."

Rorek already knew how the Mayan calendar was divided into eighteen months. He had landed in the seventh month, that of Yaxkin: and Mol, the eighth, could not be so far away. Content suffused him.

He was so contented that he relaxed his dignity before the emperor for the first time. "I thank thee, O Za Ramna," he said, "for the sight of thy daughter has quickened the spring in my heart. She is fair to look upon. I would see more of her!"

"One may neither see nor speak to her until after the month of Yaxkin. It is forbidden."

THE RED-HAIRED ONE had seated himself on the platform, alongside the plump little emperor. They were alone, and so Za Ramna took no offense; he was not looking for trouble with the Unknown; so he said: "Where did you come from, my friend?" He had the diplomacy of age and power.

"From Vineland." (This was the Norse name for Greenland.)

"And where is that?"

"Beyond the great ocean."

"How did you travel?"

"I suppose you'd call it a canoe."

Rorek already had learned that the limit of the Mayans' ship-building abilities lay in scooping out a log and floating in it along their narrow rivers and artificial canals.

"How far is this country of yours—this Vineland?"

Rorek was at a loss how to tell. In fact, it was rather hazy in his own mind as to how far from home he was. "It has taken us eighteen months to get here," he said.

While that was a year and a half to a Norseman it was only a year to a Mayan, for the latter had eighteen months in his calendar. Still Za Ramna was impressed. "Eighteen months!" he commented. "Did you row in your canoe all that time?"

"No. North we stopped, and there Hjalmar—" Rorek was about to tell of the death of Hjalmar at the hands of the northern redskins, but he thought better of it. He thought it unwise to mention anything that might suggest death by natives. There were a great many thousands of those royal jaguar-skinned soldiers. In their disciplined way, under sway of their ruler, they might not be so dangerous as one wild redskin, so long as the ruler was friendly; still—

"We were thirty-two when we left home," Rorek went on, "and we are only seven now. The storms have taken the rest. Sometimes on the great ocean the wind is terrible."

Za Ramna had never seen a storm at sea. It did not interest him. What did interest him was the genealogy and importance of this young man.

"Your father?" he asked bluntly, "Is he in Vineland?"

"Aye! My father is the King of Vineland and of Iceland!"

"Ah! The king!" Za Ramna's eyes beamed. "His name?"

"Ha-Aton!"

"King Ha-Aton—I salute you in the person of your son!"

Za Ramna clapped his hands loudly. A slave appeared and he ordered cups of *mishla* to be brought. This was great news indeed, all that he could ask for. He was entertaining royalty, the son of a neighboring king—even if eighteen months away; and his problem was safely solved. This stranger made no claim to divinity. No danger of his waving the sacred name of Ra-Mu in the ears of a credulous populace—or of his working magic to gain power.

Now all was understandable. The apparition of the stranger seemed quite plausible to the earthly and settled mind of Za Ramna. He could be at peace again. There was nothing supernatural here.

Handing Rorek a cup carved of chalcedony and filled with the distilled essence of the cactus marrow, he lifted another himself and drank the health of the King of far Vineland.

Rorek knew the potency of the liquor from observation. He feared to drink, yet he must be polite. He touched his lips to the draft, which was nearly as thick as honey and almost as sweet. Then he set it down.

"Drink! Drink!" mumbled the old emperor. "The son of my friend, King Ha-Aton, is welcome to Maya—welcome to the house of Za Ramna!" Za Ramna downed another cup with manifest pleasure; and ultimately dropped off to slumber on his platform, content that the one great problem of his reign had been peacefully solved.

8

A PLOT IN THE DARK

ROREK SAT FOR a while on the edge of the platform revolving in his hand the lovely chalcedony cup—an exquisite carving. Slowly he let the *mishla* run out upon the floor. For a time the snoring of the emperor was the only sound in the soft tropic night.

Presently another came to him—a *"tck!"* from a recess behind the platform. At first he paid no attention and then he saw a hand beckoning. He watched the hand until he felt that he recognized it. Was it not the hand of Taycapin?

Finally her head appeared and she beckoned to him. The moment he had gone beyond view of the platform she seized his garment—the worn wolfskin of his tunic—and pulled him into a room that ran along the far side of the palace.

With fluttering hands she dismissed two of her women who were there. Then she beamed on Rorek with her dark eyes.

"O Quetzalcoatl!" she exclaimed, "it has seemed an eternity since I was alone with you!"

"Where is your husband—I mean your husbands?" Rorek snapped.

"Pouf! They are nothing. They were before I knew you.

And now that we are alone, there is no time to be lost. Za Ramna sleeps—his sleep is heavy—the time is come—"

Rorek had no means of knowing what was in her mind, despite the fact that she seemed to assume he needed no further explanation from her.

"The time?" he stammered. "Time for what?" Perhaps he was embarrassed. Who could tell? It was quite dark.

She saw she must prepare his mind more fully. After all he was stupid—merely a man; yet he was the medium through whom she must work—the instrument placed to her hand. She must be patient with him and explain.

"Listen, Quetzalcoatl!" she began.

"Aye, princess!"

"I am Taycapin—your Taycapin," she went on tensely, while Rorek mopped the moist sweat from his brow. "You are to know it is just that you should come to me from our great ancestor, Ra-Mu. I have heard what you have told Za Ramna. That is a very good clever little story, but you and I know the truth. You are Ra-Mu."

"No, princess! I am the son of Ha-Aton, King of—"

"Hush, Quetzalcoatl, heir of Ra-Mu. Listen: It is Mayan law that no woman shall sit upon the throne of Ra-Mu, else would I long ago have done the deed I urge upon you tonight—for that Za Ramna has no direct male heir. He has forty wives and no son." She laughed with bitter sarcasm. "Now do you understand?"

"Understand what?"

"How the gods have sent you here—to me—to Taycapin, a daughter of Ra-Mu, that you may sit with me upon the throne of my fathers, and that I may be your empress and rule with you the land that was ours before—"

Rorek moved a bit. The moon was falling through a high window and he wanted her face to come under it so he might study it the better. He thought she must surely be mad.

He did study it, and he saw an olive oval of singular strength. Her nose was of aquiline perfection, the line of her throat of exquisite contour, but her eyes were close set, and just now they seemed like two great black coals blazing in somber depths. He said nothing.

"Now, you understand," she insisted.

"No. I have told the emperor about my father, the king—"

Swiftly she placed her cool tiny hand across his large mouth. "I heard you. Because you have told him is one reason we must strike at once. On the morrow he will proclaim from the plaza that you are from a land across a sea, the son of a brother emperor, a mere guest of the house of Ra-Mu. Then the people will no longer think you are divine."

"Will that do any harm?" asked Rorek, drawing her out.

"Harm?" hissed the princess. "It would destroy us at once. Maya will accept no one as ruler save Ra-Mu—and his sons."

"And suppose I do not wish to rule these little men?"

HER THIN LIPS closed—a straight line. Then she said, slowly, between set teeth: "But you will, my Quetzalcoatl— you will want to rule. There is a blessing in ruling—the greatest joy on earth. And it is thine—with me!"

She lifted her face to his and offered herself subtly to him. He looked at her coolly.

She stamped her tiny foot angrily. "Stupid!" she cried.

"The night passes. It is our chance—our one chance. If we strike now and in the morning it is seen in Maya that Za Ramna is no more, then I, Taycapin, the eldest survivor of the house, will announce that our father god has sent his son, our own Ra-Mu, from across the sea, to rule the children of Maya—and you will ascend the throne of Maya, and I will he on your right hand—your empress!"

Rorek looked at her as if he still had to be convinced.

She reached forth her hand swiftly. "Let me see your dagger," she demanded.

He watchfully handed her the iron knife with which he had shattered the obsidian *pecate* of the priest Pocapa Tlal. She ran her thumb over its edge and handed it back with a covert sneer. Then from her bosom she drew a thin, short knife of bone, and gave it to him. Its edge was honed until it could slit a hair.

"With that," she said, pointing toward the other room whence the royal snores could be heard. "Quickly!"

Rorek gasped, "But he is your brother!"

"He is not yours! Hasten!"

She began urging him forward gently. At his side she murmured, "O Quetzalcoatl! Emperor of Maya!"

ROREK WENT BACK into the room where Za Ramna slept on the raised platform. The emperor was on his back, and, by means of a slight glow from a charcoal brazier which was alight in one corner, Rorek could distinguish his fleshy features; the jowls relaxed, the paunch rising and heaving and subsiding like waves. He was evidently enjoying the aftereffects of *mishla* in a customary manner—and rather noisily.

Rorek was a Norseman and a fighter of experience.

When he had first set eyes on Za Ramna, he had, without conscious thought, appraised the man swiftly, in a fighter's fashion. He had decided that if he ever chose to strike, with arrow, sword, or knife, he would aim at the thick jugular vein in the neck. The ruler was too meaty around the heart; and the bones of his head looked thick, The neck was the place.

But he was not thinking of that as he toyed with the effeminate bone knife in his strong hand. He was thinking of the Viking law of hospitality, inbred in his royal being. He was thinking of Taycapin, well past her first youth, and of her four husbands. And that made him think of a slender feminine figure, riding an unfamiliar sort of beast—a slender, lovely figure half robed by the clinging *huitzin*.

Here lay the sire of Za Chel!

Rorek the raider thought of the power that Taycapin had promised would be his for the seizing—and with an enigmatic smile he poked his hard fist into the ribs of the sodden, sleeping Emperor of Maya.

Za Ramna grunted in his drunken sleep and turned over. That was all. Rorek had meant to wake him and make any attempt on his life impossible; but Mayan *mishla* proved more potent than a Norse fist.

At once two figures glided into the room—a slave on guard from the corridor, and Taycapin from where she had been impatiently waiting.

Rorek joined Taycapin while the slave approached his royal master and found him still slumbering.

"He stirred and alarmed the guard, princess, as I was about to strike," Rorek murmured, watching Taycapin as they went into the outer room. The servant had quietly returned to his post in the corridor.

"Oh-h!" There was bitter reproof in her tone.

"Now it is too late," Rorek said with assumed regret.

"It is not too late!" she insisted, sternly, holding him by the hand and thrusting into the other a stone manikin which she had seized from a niche in the wall. "Beat out his brains with this!"

Rorek wisely took charge of the stone object, and again the ambitious Taycapin began shoving him toward the emperor's room. He moved far too slowly to please her. As he reached the lintel, his foot caught, apparently, and the stone manikin dropped from his hands to the stone flags of the floor—with a crash.

"By Ah Buch!" Taycapin cried, invoking the Lord of Death. "You are a brainless churl, and neither god nor man. In my folly I called you Quetzalcoatl," she sneered. "Plumed serpent! Ha! A buzzard rather! A worn jackal! Pretender! I will have you torn to bits and thrown to my dogs!"

She was gone, leaving him alone in the chamber of Za Ramna, who at last had awakened and was sitting upright.

"Is it you, my friend?" mumbled Za Ramna.

"Aye, Za Ramna."

"Where is the sleep of my house—has it not come to you?"

"Aye. Be not disturbed."

"Good. It is well to sleep."

A moment later the contented emperor was again on His back, mouth wide open, and it seemed to Rorek that the echoes of his slumber must be heard to Mayapan.

PRESENTLY ROREK HEARD a series of low sounds from the niche beyond the emperor—the place whence the guards had appeared when called, and to which they had retired when finished with their duties around the person of their master. They seemed like moans, and he started to his feet.

A few moments later Taycapin again beckoned from the far shadows. The moon was up now and rendered a dim light. Watchfully Rorek went to her in her adjoining chamber. Without a word she took him by the hand, led him around by a back way to the long, narrow space devoted to the guards, and there thrust him forward.

Rorek stumbled over the body of one of the guards, who did not move. Rorek went to his knees. The man was dead. His throat had been cut. Two companions, near by, likewise wallowed in their blood.

He rose and confronted Taycapin, who still held in her hand the little knife she had given Rorek and which she had taken from him when he first failed to use it.

"Look there," she said, pointing down tensely, "and see what must be done to seize a throne!"

"Woman, why kill these slaves?"

"They are the emperor's favorites! They and the emperor alone stood between you and—destiny!"

"You did this?"

"I, Taycapin—a woman!" She stood febrile and taut, gazing at him with superb insolence. At that moment his military sense told him that she was far more fit to command that jaguar army than her fat-paunched brother who lay supine a few feet beyond. Yet he felt as if he were closeted with some strange venomous reptile.

He seized her hand—the hand that held the knife. Slowly she unclasped it, and he took the knife from her, and looked at it. Yes, it was smeared with blood.

She led him back to the room where the stone manikin lay. This she picked up, as she urged, "Now you have one more chance to prove you are Quetzalcoatl—you need have no fear of interruption. Strike and strike well! His guards will never hear him call!"

"But the city beyond—his army!" Rorek protested angrily.

"Bah! Do you ask first that Taycapin slit the throats of him and all his jaguar-skins? What are you? The running shadow of a jackdaw? Come! Strike!"

He took her by the shoulder. It was the first time he had ever touched her, and she was surprised to feel his strength. It suffused her as though she had imbibed a cup of *mishla*—the stark male power of him. No jackdaw this, nor jackal, either!

She flowed in upon him, and her breast touched his—until he held her off rudely.

"You lied to me yesterday," he asserted coldly. His mind had been searching for some way to turn this woman from her murderous plans, and this had occurred to him.

"I, Taycapin, lie?"

"You lied when you told me that she—Za Chel—was going to be sacrificed."

"Za Chel?" Jealousy flamed in Taycapin's breast. "An empire at stake, and you waste breath on that chit of a girl—a nobody—a virgin to save maize for the people."

"Her father said she is not to be sacrificed."

"Not now—later. It is written."

He cupped her chin in one huge hand and lifted it up into the moonlight where he could see her face clearly, to read the dark secrets hidden there, if possible. "What is that? Explain."

She stamped her foot impatiently.

"As the Chief Virgin of the Sun, she must be given to the well if the next harvest is not right."

"Ah—if!"

Taycapin sneered. "The next harvest never is right. Who ever heard of the people having all the maize they want?"

Rorek looked at her long, so long and so mistily that she came to believe his mood must be romantic. She felt the rigor of his clasp relax, and she relaxed. Finally she said softly, "Before long it will be dawn. Come, beloved— strike him!"

STILL HE HELD back, on the threshold of the royal chamber. She seized the stone manikin firmly in her hand and advanced. "If you do not settle him with the knife, I will do it—with this!" She brandished the ugly, pointed object.

Rorek straightened. He could no longer temporize with Taycapin, for all that she had befriended him. As the royal guest of a royal house, he had but one honorable course.

In another moment the Norseman was standing by the couch of Za Ramna, calling stoutly on him to get up; and in his hand he held her own knife against the princess.

Za Ramna stirred at last, blinked, and rubbed his bleary eyes.

"What is it, my friend?" he drowsily queried.

"Rise, Za Ramna! Your life is in danger!"

This thought registered. The plump little ruler got his

feet firmly on the stone and began bellowing for his guard. None arrived.

"Save your breath," said Rorek. "You have no guard!"

"Guards! Guards!" yelled Za Ramna again.

"Your guard is slain!"

Za Ramna would not believe it until he went into the antechamber and saw the gory spectacle with his own eyes.

Meanwhile the Princess Taycapin, erect and tense as the stone she held in her hand, did not move. Her mouth was a slit of purpose; her eyes two live beads of black.

The emperor demanded: "Who did this?"

Rorek pointed to the woman regretfully and half apologetically, "Your sister, O emperor."

"What! Taycapin? You infernal witch!"

Still she did not open her mouth.

Za Ramna, his mind still confused by the fumes of alcohol, turned to Rorek. "You saw her do this?" he asked.

"No, Za Ramna; but look!" He exhibited the knife.

Za Ramna looked at the knife and drew back, startled.

Taycapin said, with the softest of sneers, "The knife is in his hand, my brother."

"Why kill my guards?" Za Ramna demanded now, his choler rising.

Taycapin sneered. "Come with me. I will show you the murderers."

Za Ramna waddled after her, and Rorek came on behind, on the alert.

At the rear entrance to the palace, on the high stone approach, the Norse archers were sleeping. It was not a comfortable perch, but that did not deter them from hearty slumber after their long day's march and their feats with the buckler throne. Each of the six was sound asleep. The moonlight bathed them in ghostly radiance, but clearly revealed them.

Taycapin paused above the nearest, Eric, and pointed down, "hook!" she said.

Za Ramna and Rorek followed her finger. Eric's tunic was smeared with blood. And also that of Olav, who slept next. And Wolfkin's, the third. Their three swords were red with blood.

"These slaves of thy 'friend,'" she asserted coldly, "murdered your guard. You were to be next. I saved your life, and the wily snake accuses me!"

9

A TIGHT PLACE

ONE MOMENT NOW of indecision and Rorek would be lost—a convicted assassin in the hands of a strange people.

"Up! Eric!" He waited not for his voice alone, but delivered also a swift kick at his chief archer, lying there in such apparent guilt beside his bloody sword.

"Up! Olav! Donal! Wolfkin! Hemnet! Galko!" He called them one by one.

They leaped up, armed, almost as one. Fortunately their share of the welcoming *mishla* was being held for them against the feast of the coming morrow. They had retired ill-fed, and now were gaunt, alert, ready to die—if need be—fighting.

A ring of long steel closed in Za Ramna and Taycapin.

"Not a sound from you!" mapped Rorek at the two Mayans.

It all happened with such astonishing celerity that the befuddled despot had no time to collect his thoughts, and there was no precedent for such a thing as this. The guards who slept near him were servants, nothing more. He had never been in danger before, except from the snakes and beasts of the jungle. His jaw sagged in pure surprise as he looked around at the blond giants.

Taycapin was not fuddled, however. With the sword of Wolfkin not six inches from her breast, she spoke calmly to her brother.

"Make no outcry or we are lost."

This seemed strangely playing into the hand of Rorek, but the tense little woman went on evenly, speaking apparently only to her brother, but her eyes sought those of Rorek. She fixed the Norseman with her steady, hypnotic glare, and he realized that she had the audacity to continue her plot for power in the crux of this tight moment when all seemed lost for her—pleading with him to carry on the intrigue she had proposed, the imperial assassination, and seizure of the throne.

And she did it all in the guise of solicitude for her brother!

"For if you die, who in Maya would doubt he was Ra-Mu come again across the great waters?" she softly, almost caressingly, intoned to her brother, though eying Rorek to see how far her insinuation had gone with him. "With the last male of the reigning line dead, who would there be to carry on the power and glory of Maya save only this strong stranger?"

Za Ramna saw the force of her argument, saw it clearly. But he had known Taycapin for a long time. Now, in his extremity, while his *mishla*-filled stomach heaved with his emotion and the sweat stood forth on his fleshy head, he turned on her and asked, "How came your knife in his hand?"

Rorek made the answer for her, and it was not direct. He made it by taking from the hand of Eric the good, broad, long Norse sword. He passed it to the emperor, hilt fore-most.

"Look, O Za Ramna," said he. "Observe where the blood lies."

Za Ramna took the sword of the chief archer, while the blades of Eric's comrades yet hemmed him in; and he examined it close to the charcoal brazier so he might miss nothing.

There was much blood, but it was smeared just below the hilt, halfway down the shaft. It stopped well short of the point and lay not on the cutting edges.

"Your sword, Olav! And yours, Wolfkin!" Rorek took the two others which were red, leaving still three on guard. He passed them in turn to Za Ramna. Even as on the sword of the chief archer, the blood was palpably on them not from use.

"See, my friend," Rorek continued, "these swords are innocent. They have not been used to-night, but some designing plotter has sought to place on them the blame for that which they know not. A plotter," and he smiled, "who knows little of the ways of Norsemen's swords."

ZA RAMNA EXAMINED each of the others as carefully as he had the first. Then he returned them to Rorek, without comment. Rorek, in turn, placed them again in the hands of his archers.

Za Ramna was of royal blood; he was without coward-ice, yet he was equally without decision, for even now he made none, but waited, to let events flow over him—and through him, as they must, he being Za Ramna, august and mighty, the single will regnant in Maya.

He did not press for an answer to the question he had

addressed to Taycapin; he made no more of the accusation she had hurled at Rorek. He merely looked from one to another.

Rorek took the thing in hand himself—by calling sharply, "Eric, and all of you—sheathe your swords at once!"

"Aye, Rorek!"

"Retire—and await orders!"

"Aye, Rorek!"

The archers returned to their stone couch.

Za Ramna, Taycapin and Rorek were alone in the imperial chamber. The emperor sat down and sighed. Here was another hard decision to make. What should he do? It was clear the stranger was an innocent man. Yet he could scarcely believe that his sister could be guilty. Even if she were guilty, what then could he do? She was too old for a sacrifice, for the gods had no use for a married woman.

Taycapin came to his rescue. She hated him because he had been born a boy and she a girl; yet she ruled him.

"Ramna," she said curtly, "I will remain no longer in the palace while you subject yourself to such danger."

"Danger? From whom?"

"If you don't see it now, idiot, you will never see it. I bid you farewell, At dawn I start for Mayapan."

"Ah! Very well!"

So Taycapin went—and the emperor let her slip from his fingers, while Rorek said nothing. He felt she was going to the ancient capital for the sole purpose of linking her forces with those of the High Priest, Pocapa Tlal. He was tempted for a moment to urge her brother to detain her, but thought better of it. No use to ask Za Ramna to take any sort of action.

As she left the chamber he handed her the knife, without a word. She took it, and gave him a swift, tense look. Was it malevolent? Or still pleading? In the moonlight, which rendered her palely beautiful, he could not be sure what she meant.

When she had gone, Rorek felt as if the dynamic force of the empire had departed. It was clear that drink, sleep and ease were all that Za Ramna asked of life.

THE NEXT AFTERNOON, at the hour of the Sparrow, which was just when the shadows began to lengthen, four heralds appeared on the steps of the palace, each bearing a ram's horn, which they blew in unison.

The populace began drifting into the plaza, where the jaguar soldiers were previously assembled. The soldiers guarded the spaces about the palace steps to keep them clear. Soon in all directions an enormous crowd spread—many thousands of people.

In due time Za Ramna appeared, accompanied by Rorek. He held up his hand for silence and addressed his people. "The son of my friend, Ha-Aton, the king of the good people across the great waters, has come to sojourn with us for a while. See to it that his paths are pleasant and his hours filled only with gladness."

A great shout went up, but in it Rorek could hear a little murmuring undertone which carried up two names—Ra-Mu and Quetzalcoatl—the name Taycapin had given him, and of the legendary name of the founder of the reigning house of Maya.

He stepped forward and lifted his hand, for he felt the auspiciousness of the occasion. "Friends in Maya!" he cried,

"I come in peace—to greet my friend, your great Emperor! *Skoal!*"

He reached up his two hands, high above his red head, and shook them. It was a gesture strange to the crowd, yet the people gathered his meaning. They laughed and shouted in response, and many lifted their hands.

Then came the great feast. All day the peccaries brought by Taycapin had been steaming. This was a much more marvelous feast than Taycapin offered on the edge of the jungle. In addition to the peccaries there were huge pots containing a pudding made of *teocentli,* or the sacred maize grown in the cloud-land, and others containing the mashed *manioc* spiced with peppers and cacao.

There were fried bananas—fried on hot stones until the sweet juices ran—and persimmons plucked of seeds, and strawberries served in honey, with jellied guavas and avacodos, and many nuts. To say nothing of the *mishla.*

As dusk came and all seemed bursting with food and drink, little girls passed among the Rasters with a bowl of soft round brown pellets about the size of marbles. Each Mayan took one, placed it in his mouth and began chewing joyously.

Rorek asked Za Ramna what they were.

"*Yinska!*" said the emperor, who himself refrained from chewing it. So Rorek too abstained. In a few moments the effects of the *yinska* became apparent. The chewers began acting strangely.

Then Rorek learned what *yinska* was—a mixture of tobacco and cocaine fixed in chicle for chewing. One pellet was enough to send a chewer into drugged ecstasy.

Za Ramna became expansive with his *mishla.* "Now, my

friend," he said, "it is time for you to choose your wives. Look!"

A dance was forming, among the trees. Lithe maidens were advancing, retreating, darting in and out with little giggles or with repressed sighs; thrusting out their knees so that their *huipilas* stood out like tail-feathers.

"Wives?" said Rorek, "how many?"

"As many as you like," said Za Ramna generously.

Rorek contemplated this idea for a moment. Then he asked, "How about my archers? They need wives."

"Let them choose—as they like. They may live as live my jaguar soldiers. Two wives each."

So it came about that each of the six archers had two Mayan wives. But not Rorek.

10

A CRIME AGAINST THE GODS

"ZA CHEL!"

The crowds beyond the plaza were crying the name, and Rorek heard them from the Red Palace, where he had been housed by the emperor, and where his days were spent in becoming even more familiar with the words and thoughts of Maya—a sheep-like little people so different from his own Vikings that the marvel of them interested him constantly.

Rorek stepped to the edge of the palace and looked forth. The streets were packed as he had not seen them since that day he had marched in, with the jaguar soldiers everywhere lining the way.

A month had gone since he and his archers had come that way from Mayapan. A Mayan month, twenty days. It was now the middle of Mol, the month of planting. Already the rains had come and the fields were soft. The limestone walls of the palaces were washed clean and the bright colors shone from them with gay splendor.

Now he could see, far in the distance, the head of the procession, for it was no single figure now approaching— no single svelte girl on a lone llama. This was a great ceremonial parade.

Across, on the steps of the Imperial Palace, Rorek saw Za Ramna appear, but not as he had ever seen him before. Now the emperor was panoplied for some great purpose. He wore an elaborate collar of shell and jade that reached down over his breast; great armlets of turquoise. The emerald of Cochibar glittered in the middle of his forehead, and above it an extensive headdress, massive and awe-inspiring, was topped with a mass of *quetzal* feathers. The royal *huitzin* fell from his shoulders, and from his heels, like spurs, rose tufts of copper-colored feathers.

The emperor of Maya was going forth to impress the gods, especially the Long-nosed God of Rain, for the season had arrived when the God of Rain was all-important. There was rejoicing in Uxmal, and all the other cities of Maya, for the Chief Virgin of the Sun had spent her month of penitence and lonely vigil at Chichen Itza wisely and well. Thrice in the past week the heavens had opened and the Long-nosed God had poured forth his generous gifts to the fields of Maya.

It was a fine beginning, but there must be more, much more, rain, that the maize and the pumpkins, and the squash, and the beans might prosper and ripen in the long valleys.

As Za Ramna appeared and stepped forth into the way that he might greet the returning virgin, the conch shells shrilled. Then rams' horns sounded long and loud through the streets. And, instantly thereafter, there was a vast rattle of drums and droning of flageolets.

As the Sun Virgin passed, those nearest threw themselves into the dirt, abased their faces and averted their eyes. "Za Chel! Za Chel!" they murmured.

Ah Puch, the Lord of Death, would touch them if they dared profane her with their near glance.

But Ah Puch was not in Rorek's pantheon. He saw a maiden lovelier than any dream—black hair, hazel eyes, light olive skin. The same he had seen that day near Mayapan, but there was something added to her now. Then her head had been down, her eyes averted, her soul had seemed in a mist. Now a radiance beamed from her whole person. She was alight with triumph—the triumph of an accomplished purpose. For had she not traveled alone to the great well at Chichen Itza—the horrible well—and had she not, alone there with the Long-nosed God, prevailed on him to favor the sons of Maya?

Za Chel was returning in glory to her temple. Rorek remembered the malign predictions of Taycapin, and was glad that the ambitious princess was not in Uxmal—glad that he had so deftly and surely circumvented her evil designs.

THIS TIME ZA CHEL did not ride a llama, regarded in Maya as a beast to be used only for the humble. She had gone in all humility to pray for rain. The rain had come. Now she—and Maya—were rich. So she returned in a mahogany litter suspended across the backs of two tame jaguars.

Rorek took firm hold of his sword as he saw the great jungle cats slide along the street, glancing with feline stealth from side to side, while the radiant girl rode the litter on their backs. If one should turn to rend her—

Rorek did not know that the claws and the teeth of the jaguars had been pulled the night before, tame though they were, for not the least chance could be taken with the safety of the virgin.

As Za Chel came nearer the plaza the drums and flageolets burst into a fury of acclaim. Za Ramna, riding ahead, stopped at the foot of the steps to the temple, and stepped aside to let the virgin go on up to the place of her abode. Even he bowed as she passed. Even he, Za Ramna, dared not speak to her. Thus sacred was she, Chief Virgin of the Sun.

Now Rorek saw her on the top step of the temple, in the sunlight. Her little breasts were circled with chaplets of gold. The wondrous Yellow Sapphire of Itzamna, the Father God, held the fire of the sun at her neck, where it danced superbly.

The sacred *huipila*, of yellow bound with sapphire blue, was around her waist. From her shoulders depended the *huitzin*, soft and luminous in the molten light. High from her dark tresses rose a stiff headdress of jade, every piece of which was pierced, and from each tiny hole flew a *quetzal* feather, copper-colored, so that with each movement of her head the feathers rippled in cascades of beauty.

She was a symphony in sun colors, yellows and coppers, with flashes of blue and green. As Rorek looked on her she seemed the very orb of life itself.

In a moment she was gone within the temple, followed by the women who attended her, and then the flageolets began a weird and mournful incantation, while the drums began popping a dreadful funeral-like pounding that kept up on through the night.

Later, as Rorek ate with Za Ramna, in the imperial

apartments, he reminded the emperor of his promise that he should meet and talk with the virgin.

"Later," said Za Ramna.

"When?" Rorek was insistent.

"After the harvest."

"After the harvest—many months!"

"And then—only perhaps."

"Perhaps? But I want to see her to-night—or, at least, to-morrow."

A very stern look came into the face of Za Ramna. "It is against the law of Maya!" he asserted, and would not return to the subject.

Rorek retired presently to the Red Palace for the night. The Red Palace lay between the Yellow Palace and the temple. His archers, all of whom were now married, with two wives apiece, were living in palm-thatched huts just beyond the Red Palace. There were no other guards. What was there to prevent his going over to the temple?

He would not go up the front steps where he might be seen.

TO THINK WAS to act with Rorek, especially in an affair like this. It was a dark night. Avoiding the open spaces he found his way through rear streets until he stood beyond the temple, on the far side, which he had not seen before.

Here was a projection, a building of flat walls, all stone, and very high. In the dark he could find no entrance and could see no windows. For the moment he was baffled.

Then, almost in his face, a door opened, and a dusky figure came out, leaving the door ajar. Flat against the wall he was not seen, but could distinguish the figure. It was that of a woman, one of the temple attendants. Out of the dark beyond, she was joined by a man and the two drew aside.

Rorek slipped in through the half open door.

Inside he found a rectagonal stairway. He followed it up to what must be the main floor. He came into a room lit by a single charcoal brazier. He paused for a moment to get used to the light and at length distinguished half a dozen or more female forms—all asleep. He passed through to the room beyond.

He had studied the temple from the outside. It was built in a form similar to that of the palaces, like all the Mayan public buildings, and now he found that its interior arrangement was similarly simple. In the rear there were only three rooms. He passed through the rearmost and came to the central chamber.

In the door he paused to get accustomed to the dim light. Here were two charcoal braziers. From their soft glow he at length distinguished the platform across the room. He advanced to it, and sat down on the edge.

Za Chel lay with her head on her arm, sleeping. For a long time Rorek looked at her, entranced. He thought not to wake her. He dared not, for fear she might cry out; yet he longed to talk with her.

Finally, she must have felt an alien presence. She stirred and came to a sitting posture, swiftly, with the ease of a little animal accustomed to the wild.

She reached out and touched him to be sure that he was real, then darted back to the far shadows of the platform, in fright, but placed her hand quickly to her mouth to suppress an involuntary cry.

"Be not afraid!" he whispered, "it is I, Rorek, the Norse."

He spoke in Mayan and the wonder of this seemed to calm her. Of course she had heard of him. Who in Maya had heard of much else the past month?

"Oh! Quetzalcoatl!" she murmured, her initial fright oozing away. It was the name her aunt, Taycapin, had given him. That augured well.

"If I had the wisdom of the serpent and the beauty of the flying bird and the strength of the prowling jaguar, then I would use them all to come to you." Rorek went on tensely.

"But it is forbidden!"

"Who forbids?"

"The gods!"

"My gods are not thy gods!"

She gave a soft little cry almost of alarm at this. It seemed to estrange them.

"But I love your gods, because they are yours," he added quickly.

"Then fly at once, before they know you are here."

"I must talk with you first."

"It is death—"

"But I must!"

SHE CAME NEARER to him now and leaned very close, and he could see the clean, strong oval of her face, the purity of its outline, like Taycapin's, but with the roundness of youth. "Go!" she implored, "before it is too late!"

"Tell me," he insisted, "why it is we may not see each other before the harvest."

"I am the First Virgin of the Sun," she replied simply, with a regal tilt to her head, as if that settled it.

"But I do not understand. It is you and you alone in all Maya I want to see. I must see you—often."

The charcoal gave little light, yet he could perceive she was frightened at this, though she respected him as a stranger and as one worthy to be known as the Plumed Serpent.

"No. That cannot be," she shook her head.

"But why?"

"Because I am a hostage to Ah Bolan Dzacab."

Rorek recognized Ah Bolan as the God of Rain.

"You have been successful. The rains have come."

"The first rains, yes. But there must be more. If they come and the harvest is good, then all is well. Perhaps, if Za Ramna approves. I can see you then."

"Suppose it does not rain."

"Then I must give myself to Ah Bolan Dzacab in the well at Chichen Itza."

"That is horrible!" Rorek was aghast.

"It is the law of Maya."

She said it simply, and with utter finality.

He had sensed something of this. Intuition had told him what he had to meet. Long before this he had heard of the sacrifices of the fairest maidens of Maya in the Dread Well at Chichen Itza. He had thought of little else for days.

Now he leaned toward the virgin.

"Listen, Za Chel," he said, whispering, for the women still slept in the room beyond, "will you care to know how I came to Maya—how I, Rorek, son of the King Ha-Aton, came to realize this fairest of all dreams—to see you, lovely Goddess of the Sun?"

She made a little sound, mingled of modest protest and interest.

He went on. "In my country, too, the king is obliged,

on certain occasions, to sacrifice his eldest. I am the eldest son of the king. For long his people were in ill luck. The storms wiped out their vessels; the cattle would not breed; the chiefs who went to foray came back empty-handed. The people demanded a sacrifice, and I was chosen to be given to our Norse gods."

A little gasp told him his audience was with him. Za Chel crept on the platform until she was close to him. Her deep eyes clung to his tenaciously. She scarcely breathed.

No word was necessary to ask him to proceed.

"The king, my father," Rorek continued, "called for me one day, and told me to prepare for a long journey. He did not tell me where it was to be, but when the preparations were done I knew.

"I was to be taken across a narrow sea to a headland and there, in sight of all the people, offered to the gods as a sacrifice—"

"Killed?"

"Aye! On a stone altar."

Za Chel remained silent, in a deathlike concentration on his words.

The soft tones of Rorek now filled the chamber. "I set forth to the sacrifice. Thirty-two men rowed me in the finest vessel in Vineland; but no sooner had we left the land than a great storm arose. Despite the best efforts of the rowers the vessel was blown out to sea. When the storm lifted we were beyond sight of land. We kept on and on. After many months we came to Maya. And so—"

"Sssh!" She touched him, softly, on the arm. There was a noise from the adjoining room. "Go!" she said. "You could not escape so easily in Uxmal!"

Rorek heard talk and frightened scurries. He went to the door and looked. None of the women were in the adjoining room. He crossed it and came to the head of the stairs.

Then the guards leaped on him, from behind.

He fought like a great bear. He was stronger than five, than ten, but not stronger than fifty or a hundred. In a short time they had him, bound with gnarled jungle vines, on the ground behind the temple.

11

THE STONE OF SACRIFICE

IT WAS THE hour before dawn. Rorek, bound with copious windings of giant creeper, the tough, gnarled vines of the jungle, lay helpless at the base of the projecting house in the rear of the temple. He could see between the nearest palm-thatched huts toward the east the first pale gray hint of light.

The Sun God was coming. To aid or to destroy?

The vines almost strangled him as he lay panting, worn with his struggles. He could see the evil, half-scared faces of the jaguar soldiers who stood above him.

They would scurry away in confusion when his legs moved, or his body writhed, and yet always enough held the vines, which were cinched tight, to prevent him from struggling free of the enfolding clasp.

He was like Gulliver imprisoned by the Lilliputians. Only an army of them could have subdued him, yet he gasped in dire suffering as his continued attempts to free himself caused them to close in upon him the more stiflingly.

Evidently many of them still believed him to be divine, for, every once in a while, one would shout, "See! he is only a man!" Then he would sneak up to Rorek's ear and

"Ska-na!" the Vikings roared their war-cry.

give it a fierce pull, at which Rorek would curse and pull away. Whereupon, with a squeak of reassurance to each other, they would withdraw and discuss this evidence of his mortality.

They would kick him in the side, and cinch the creepers across his groin to hear him protest. Pygmies jubilant with their power over a giant. In fact, he stood only two feet taller than most of them; but when he had stood before, it had seemed a mile to many of them.

Now he was supine and the bullying cruelty of their natures was given full vent.

They might have killed him there before dawn by infinitesimal degrees of torture, except that a puma-clad official from Mayapan constantly intervened, with a hoarse warning, "Beware! If he be not alive for the coming of the high priest, one in three of you will be seized for Ah Bolan Dzacab!"

That restrained them to little tortures—little tweaks of

the ear, little punches in the stomach, little twists of the arms, little ticklings on the ball of the foot.

Rorek soon realized he was using up his strength to no avail, and desisted from movement or curses, and lay still as if unconscious.

This stopped them. The captain came up and examined him. The half light was struggling through the early clouds. He became alarmed until he seized a feather from a near-by standard and held it under Rorek's nose and saw it move slightly with his breath.

Then the captain rose and uttered his judgment sternly to his soldiers: "He is no God. On peril of your lives do not touch him more. Beware the wrath of Ah Bolan Dzacab."

WHEN THE LIGHT grew stronger and before the rim of the sun appeared above the horizon, a flutter of commotion beyond the plaza apprised the spent Rorek that some one of importance was approaching. He opened his eyes.

In the early light he clearly saw a familiar advancing figure. An obese form, ugly, squat, powerful, striding toward him with firm confident steps, and flanked by two marching columns of the puma-clad soldiers.

It was Pocapa Tlal, come from Mayapan to officiate in the dread judgment of the Sun God on this impious outlander who had dared address the Sun Virgin.

Just beyond Pocapa Tlal, lounging in her litter, with her headdress piled six inches above her scalp to indicate the height of her authority, reclined the audacious Taycapin.

They had started the day before to bring obeisance to Za Chel in return for her successful importuning of the well, had camped on the edge of the city at sundown, and there, past the middle of the night, had received the astounding tidings that the daring stranger had invaded the sacred precincts of the holy temple—had dared enter the inner sleeping apartment of the virgin, where no man had ever stepped before. Not even her father, Za Ramna, holy vice-regent of the Sun God, nor the high priest himself would have dared so monstrous an outrage of all the sacred laws enforced in Maya since before the dawn of time.

At length Pocapa Tlal stood looking down into the face of the prostrate Rorek. He uttered one word, "Blasphemer!" It was the most terrible indictment he could make.

Rorek had seen the granite-like lips close as if a trap had been set. And the beady eyes glowed, like those of a reptile about to strike. Rorek fearlessly glared back, and laughed in the priest's face.

Pocapa Tlal turned and gave a few sharp commands. Rorek was lifted by a dozen of the guards and shifted to a place near the front of the temple, where he could see the great sacrificial stone which was emplaced on the second platform, halfway up the long incline of the hundred and twenty steps that led from the plaza to the door of the temple.

UP THE STEPS of the temple waddled the high priest, Pocapa Tlal. When he stood above the sacrificial stone, halfway up the hundred and twenty stone steps, he held over the altar his obsidian jaguar-and-rattle-snake manikin. It was like the *pecate* which Rorek had broken, that momentous day back at Mayapan; but stouter—as if to resist such impious assaults.

In a moment four of his puma-clad soldiers led up the long steps the sacred llama on which Rorek had seen Za

Chel that first day, long ago in the month of Vaxkin, on her way to pray at Chichen Itza.

They laid the llama on the stone. Pocapa Tlal passed over it the manikin, uttered a long prayer of supplication to Ah Bolan Dzacab, and then, with a bone knife taken from his girdle, leaned over and deftly opened the breast of the gentle beast.

The llama's piteous cries resounded through the square. The sleeping townspeople began stirring from the thatched huts into the narrow streets.

Pocapa Tlal thrust his hairy right hand into the breast of the poor llama and tore from it the living heart, which he held aloft for all to see, while the llama bleated and the blood ran. He permitted this insensate brutality to continue until the cries of the animal began to die down from exhaustion, and the llama's head drooped. Then, just as the beast was about to expire, he severed the heart and thrust it on the center of the stone.

Quickly, with deft strokes, like an accomplished butcher, Pocapa Tlal stripped the hide from the llama, whose flesh was still quivering with life barely gone. He stripped it in long thin strings, diagonally, from neck to rump, and passed them, one by one, to a waiting assistant.

In this manner eighteen strips of rawhide were obtained, fresh from the carcass of the newly killed llama. Eighteen; one for each of the Mayan months.

While all eyes were on the ceremony being carried out above on the steps of the temple, attention was diverted, for the moment, from Rorek. In the interlude Taycapin rose from her litter and approached him.

Rorek looked at her dully. The pain of the lashings which

bound him had momentarily lessened, for the guards no longer tugged on his bonds since the coming of Pocapa Tlal. Still he reclined, half sitting, helpless.

"Quetzalcoatl!" she spoke the name softly. The guards, out of respect for her royal person, had stepped back so they could not hear.

Though her tone was caressing, he looked at her face. The tiny slit of a mouth was thin as the edge of her bone knife. Her eyes were hard. He made no response.

"Fool!" she muttered. "All Maya was yours for the taking—and now you are looking on your last sun."

A thin rim of golden splendor came above the horizon as she said this, as if timed.

"It is not too late," she went on, seeing the sternly hidden suffering in his face. "Give me a sign that you will listen to me—later—and I will try to avert the judgment of the Sun God!"

He made no reply. Already the ceremony on the steps above was nearly over. The last of the strips of rawhide were being laid on the arms of his assistant by the expert Pocapa Tlal.

She bent low over Rorek.

"Quickly assure me," she whispered, "and I will try to have the officiating priest tie the bindings loosely—that you may live until sundown, and be spared. Speak—speak quickly, O Quetzalcoatl!"

He stared her in the eyes and shook his head.

The priests were coming for him. Taycapin ground her tiny heel in the soft earth viciously and turned back toward her litter.

THE PRIESTS LIFTED Rorek and carried him up the steps

and deposited him on the center of the stone altar, where the blood of the llama had not yet drained away along the sluices cut in the stone.

Thereupon, with his own hands, Pocapa Tlal began removing the bindings of the crude jungle creeper. But he was cautious to remove no more than one at a time, and he made sure that at no time he liberated the strong limbs of the stalwart and menacing giant stranger.

One after another the cumbrous jungle vines were replaced by slenderer but tougher thongs of fresh rawhide. It was a slow and tedious process which took nearly an hour, but at last it was done, and Pocapa Tlal stood back, proudly, so all could see. He gestured toward the supine victim.

But now the sun was well up. At the base of the temple and halfway up the steps crowded row on row of puma soldiers. Behind them, far along the sides of the plaza, spread the jaguar soldiers of Za Ramna. And beyond, along every street, were packed crowds of the populace.

The flageolets began to mourn. The drums patted a slow rhythmic beat. Then four heralds appeared bearing the huge ram's horns of the emperor. Lifting them high, they sounded a great blast, in unison.

Shortly, on the steps of the Yellow Palace, across the plaza, appeared Za Ramna, with the emerald of Cochibar upon his forehead, and above it a giant headdress of jade, cornelian and shell, with its flaunting *quetzal* feathers denoting his godship.

From the imperial chamber appeared two slaves bearing a stone seat, carved from lime, and decorated with bands of inset turquoise. It was the sacred witness seat where-from he would observe in royal majesty the judgment of the Sun God.

For the moment Rorek was more comfortable. He had got rid of those cumbersome bindings of jungle creeper, and, though the thongs of the fresh llama rawhide held him securely, still the change was slightly restful. Yet this was for a brief moment only.

As the emperor, in full view of his subjects and his army, became seated, Pocapa Tlal held up his hand, magisterially, and cried:

"In the name of Za Ramna, the mighty, I, Pocapa Tlal, high priest of the ruler of Maya in all the lands of the earth, here dedicate this stranger, who has willingly placed himself as a sacrifice before you, to the service of Ah Bolan Dzacab, the great Rain God, the author of our prosperity and of the fullness of our stomachs."

The obese figure, squat as a butcher, placed a hand on the stone near the head of Rorek. "Hear!" he cried. "Hear, all ye children of Maya! This sacrifice is august. He is placed beyond the knife of the High Priest by Ah Bolan Dzacab, who has asked his elder brother, the great Sun God himself, to officiate in the sacrifice. Wait! Observe! Pray!"

He waved his stout, hairy arm over Rorek's prostrate form. "Watch how the Sun God claims his sacrifice."

Already the hideousness of the torture he was facing had been borne in upon Rorek, for the strips of rawhide had begun to shrink. As they shrank, they began to cut the flesh. In six or eight hours the sun would tighten them by a fifth—and half that would mean strangulation.

As the sun rose and grew hotter on the temple steps, the fresh hide would shrivel and become taut as steel.

Now, to insure the satisfactory completion of the awesome ceremonial, which was made to appear the impersonal work of the Sun God, the officiating priests deftly fixed Rorek's body so that his neck lay just over the center of the stone, above the hollow leading to the sluice down which had just been drained the blood of the llama. And over his jugular vein they drew even more tightly two fast-drying strips of the cutting rawhide.

Rorek's mind was quite clear. The physical suffering had only begun. As he lay there, staring into the blue, he said to himself that this was the end. And an appropriate end—similar to the one his father had planned for him.

Only it was across the world. With alien peoples. In a tropic clime.

He would have preferred the bleak north cape of Greenland, and the jagged Druid stone. All of this splendor smote him with a peculiar disgust. The square huge buildings, with their ornamental colors, the serried ranks of the drilled armies, the figures of the high priest and the emperor, the sinister beauty of Taycapin, watching from the foot of the steps—these sickened him.

He closed his eyes in agony both physical and spiritual. Then he felt the first raw bite of the hide against his bare neck.

12

"SKA-NA!"

THE SUN WAS climbing the heavens—halfway to the zenith. Za Ramna sat comfortably on his witness seat. Pocapa Tlal, also, had the forethought to be provided with a seat, which had been placed at the head of the altar. There he sat, expertly observing the slow contraction of the rawhide of llama as it sank, almost imperceptibly, into the white skin of the Norseman.

The soldiers in the plaza below had relaxed their vigilance, for the lines of sight-seeing had become established, and there was no more shoving for position. The many thousands of Uxmal folk had fixed themselves for the day, to see as best they could, and to be comfortable. Vendors were going back and forth along the lines, and through the huddled streets, taking cakes and baskets of bananas and cashew nuts.

There was plentiful gossiping and laughing and low talking. Not loud, for that might prevent the Sun God and Ah Bolan Dzacab, from securing their prey which lay up there where all could see on the vast steps of the great temple, atop the bloody altar.

The drums kept up their interminable slow beat. *Boom-boom!* For hours they sounded with frightful monotony.

And the flageolets wailed on, without any cease, and without any tune—just a mournful low wail. Enough to strike terror to any strange heart. But the Mayans were used to it. They knew it was not for them, but for the victim—to cheer him on his way to Ah Bolan Dzacab.

Then, an hour before high noon, and just as the outer cuticle on the neck of Rorek was cut through and the pink had begun to appear, the door of the temple above opened. Pocapa Tlal rose. Za Ramna, across the way, rose. All the soldiers came to attention. The populace rose.

From the door, advancing slowly, appeared the Chief Virgin of the Sun. She was coming to bless the victim before his appearance at the throne of Ah Bolan Dzacab.

For this sacredly solemn moment—and for this moment alone—the High Priest withdrew. Only a few steps. Still, far enough away so that his masculine presence might not possibly contaminate the pristine purity of the personality of the Virgin.

Za Chel paused above the reclining figure of Rorek. He looked into her hazel eyes, luminous with pity.

Fortunately, the flageolets struck a more strident note—a peal of celebration of the appearance of the most precious personality in Maya. And the drums beat more wildly. Enough to drown out the sound of the voice of Za Chel.

Only the victim heard her as she softly said, "O Stranger in the land of Maya, the heart of Za Chel, the Maiden, beats with thine on the lowly sacrificial stone!"

He strove to speak, but his throat was dry. No word came.

"At sundown," she went on, gently, without any apparent emotion, as if life and death were casual incidents, "you will be safe in the land of Ah Bolan Dzacab—far in the skyland. It is well, O Stranger! Be not alarmed! But another season and I will join thee—I, Za Chel, Virgin of the Sun, will seek you in the land above! Be assured, beloved stranger!"

NOW THE SWEAT trickled into his mouth and wet his tongue. Her words seemed an answer to the desperate longing in his heart.

"Za Chel!" he whispered, while the flageolets wailed more loudly.

"Aye, Quetzalcoatl!"

"Take my dying request! May I trust you?"

"Aye, Quetzalcoatl!"

"Take word to my head archer, my Eric—do you understand?"

"Aye, Quetzalcoatl—to-morrow!"

"No. At once. To-day—now—within the half hour! Or my soul will perish!"

He saw the troubled look in her brow—the puzzled anguish. He realized he must devise a reason which would not conflict with the dictates of her religion.

"It is to propitiate my gods," he added, "that I may go to them clean and whole. I pray thee, Za Chel."

"Very well, Quetzalcoatl. It shall be at once!"

"But privately."

"Aye!" She dropped the long lashes over her eyes. "Secretly."

His heart leaped with the first note of triumph. It was a compact. He had overcome her religious scruple with an appeal to his own. She would not see him go into the other

world unshriven, if that was what he meant, as she believed
it was what he meant.

Pocapa Tlal moved as if it was time to end the ceremony.
Za Ramna shifted from one leg to another. He wanted to
sit down again.

She leaned over the victim a bit closer. "What word shall
I take?" she asked.

In his anxiety he had moved his head and the llama
hide was cutting it. With an effort of the will he remained
immovable, while his lips slowly formed the word. "*Ska-
na!*"

She repeated it—"*Ska-na!*" She did not know what it
meant—nor did any other Mayan.

In a moment she had waved above the victim her stone
wand and was gone. The doors of the temple closed on
her, and the celebrants of the day went back to their slow
waiting. The drums died down to the monotonous beat; the
flageolets whined more slowly. The populace began shuf-
fling and eating and laughing with less restraint.

No telling how long they would have to wait. This
stranger was a tough and hardy being. It might be hours
before Pocapa Tlal could announce that Ah Bolan Dzacab
had claimed his toll. It would perhaps be nearly sundown
before the high priest could open the breast of the dying
victim and take forth the bleeding heart and hold it aloft
for all to see.

Meanwhile, from the rear of the temple, out of the little
door whence the tirewomen went for their affairs in the
town, the trusted slave of Za Chel slipped softly. She made
her way through streets until she reached the little group

of houses which had been made over to the Norse archers. There she found Eric and whispered to him.

A little later, through a screen of *capa*, wood, Eric listened to the voice of the Virgin—for no man might look on her while she spoke—"I bring you one word from your master!" she whispered through the *capa* screen.

"Aye! The word?"

" *'Ska-na!'* "

"Ska-na!" He repeated it, at first slowly, and then with abrupt decision. "Aye! Assure him that Eric has the word!"

"Za Chel has spoken. Farewell!"

The slave woman plucked Eric by the tunic and ushered him into the open air. And the door closed.

"SKA-NA!" STRIKE AT once! *"Ska-na!"* meant that and more than that. It was the Norse battle cry reserved for the moment of a surprise attack. It meant not only to strike at once. It meant—strike with your whole soul, for the life of your chieftain is in danger, the safety of your home is in peril, the honor of your wives and children is at stake.

"Ska-na!"

It was the cry which aroused the final will of all Norse Vikings—the essence of all Norse fury! Those who died crying *"Ska-na!"* and fighting with their faces to the foe, went straight to Valhalla and dwelt forever there with many goddesses and oceans of fresh and foaming mead!

Eric hastened back to find the other five. They were lolling beneath the shelter of their palm-thatched huts, ready to doze through the heat of the day.

Unlike the eager and restless Rorek, they had not bothered to learn the new tongue. The wives that had been given them they had striven to teach a few words of Norse. It had not occurred to them as desirable that they should know Mayan. And so, this day, they alone in all Maya knew not that the life of the red-haired giant was being strangled away, a few squares distant, on the stone steps of the great temple.

They knew it was a day of feasting for Maya, but why they cared not. But—"*Ska-na!*" That was a clarion call.

They rose—five of them, Donal, Galko, Hemnet, Olav and Wolfkin—and joined Eric as he bound his buckler shield on his strong right arm, strapped his quiver of long arrows to his right hip, slung his long bow across his shoulder, and picked up his sword with its blade that would reach from a man's armpit to the ground.

He was Rorek's lieutenant. Silently they obeyed him. "*Ska-na!*" They welcomed the word. They were tired of lolling there with these trifling small women. It was high time for a foray.

But where should they strike, and how?

Finally accoutered, they strolled into the street and, finding the people gathered near the plaza, began pushing a way there. Shortly they came to the wall of jaguar soldiers.

But the jaguar soldiers were short—the tallest no more than four feet five inches—while Wolfkin, shortest of the archers, was five feet eight inches, and Eric, the tallest, six feet five inches. Eric towered about two feet above the line of the jaguar soldiers.

He directed the gaze of the others across the plaza, over the heads of Za Ramna's jaguar-skinned troops and then across the heads of the puma soldiers of Pocapa Tlal, to the steps of the temple, and so on up to the sacrificial altar.

The six squinted in the sun to make out what it was all about. Hemnet, the sharp-eyed, was the first to sense it.

"See!" he snarled. " 'Tis Rorek—on the stone!"

"Aye!" Eric slowly agreed. "They have him bound."

"By the hammer of Thor!" shrilled Wolfkin. "They have bound him so tight he is bleeding!"

"Pigs!" muttered Donal.

"They are many—many as leaves in the forest," growled Olav.

"If they were as many as the sands of the sea we would smite them!" cried Eric as his eyes swiftly saw where and how to strike.

Then, lifting his long sword, thrusting aloft his buckler, he cried, with a piercing shriek that had never failed to strike terror to an enemy on a foray: *"Ska-na!"*

"Ska-na!" roared the five in unison, as they attacked, the jaguar soldiers from the rear.

13

AGAINST A PYGMY MULTITUDE

THERE IS GREAT virtue in surprise. A handful of Greeks, hidden in the wooden horse, captured the armed citadel of mighty Troy. And Napoleon said: "If thousands are afraid, they are not the equal of one brave man."

So now, there were ten thousand soldiers of Pocapa Tlal in their tawny puma skins, and twenty thousand soldiers of Za Ramna in their spotted jaguar skins, and unarmed Mayans by the hundred thousand. A host, a horde, a cloud of agitated human insects.

Yet before six intrepid giants—

Eric's long sword accounted for three among the jaguar-skins with almost his first blow. That brought him through the outer rim of guards, who were acting only as police, and had no reason to anticipate so thunderous and so savage an attack.

Then came an open space, the cleared space of the plaza. He leaped across that with a mighty impetus, and the puma soldiers of the high priest at the base of the steps to the temple turned to meet him. But he had already broken through the jaguar-skins, who were everywhere accounted superior to the priest's fighters.

The puma-clad troops brought up their shields and

reached for their stone-tipped lances, but even as they reached, gaunt Eric was upon them with that terrible long, sharp sword. He laid about him with the desperation of a madman. One through the throat; another through the eye: a third in the stomach, and then, swinging it, he thumped another pair to earth with its broadside.

Only a pace behind, and no whit less terrible, plowed the five, leaping, cutting, hacking, their veins alight with the joy of battle, their souls thirsting for Valhalla, the marrow of their bones afire with berserk fury.

Za Ramna leaped to his feet and bellowed in astonished rage. "Up, army! Your arrows! Slay them!" he cried.

The inner row of jaguar-clad ones fitted their stone-tipped arrows to their little bows as fast as they could, drew them to the heads and let fly.

But they were drawn in a circle, and, before the bows could be made taut and sprung, the plaza was in a chaos of fighting and charging men; puma-skins and jaguar-skins and Norse archers all mauling away together. One flight of arrows plowed into them, but none reached its mark, and many plumped only into the backs and breasts of loyal Mayans.

The Mayan captains quickly saw they must use only lances, and so ordered.

But before even so much order could proceed among the multitudinous creatures, stout Eric had forced the inner rank of the guards of Pocapa Tlal, and was leaping, five steps at a time, up toward the sacrificial stone on the wide platform.

Between the bottom of the steps and the altar stood no one. Pocapa Tlal, at the head of the altar, armed only with his bone knife, saw the danger and cried loudly: "Shoot, archers! Shoot him now, as he runs alone!"

If one intelligent archer sharpshooter had kept his wits down there below, the tale might have been different, but so sudden had been the impact of the Norsemen that every one had been half whipped at the first blow. Moreover, there still existed a strong undercurrent of belief among the Mayans that these giant strangers were not human, but belonging to the gods.

And to strike a god—what a crime!

Pocapa Tlal saw, all too late, that the swift-running Eric would be at the altar in another moment and without interruption.

It would take quick thinking now, and swift acting, to avert this calamity which was striking at the heart of Maya. **THE HIGH PRIEST** seized boldly in his right hand the stout sacrificial knife. It had been proclaimed that the Sun God must take the life of this stranger by means of a slow strangling with the fresh rawhide, but the gods had not instructed him what to do in such a crisis as this. Pocapa Tlal did not stop to ask the gods what to do. He advanced as rapidly as his waddling fat legs would carry him to the supine man lying bound on the altar, and lifted up his knife to thrust it through the jugular.

Eric saw with unerring swiftness that he would be too late. He had still a dozen steps to climb. The knife could rise and fall and the life blood of his beloved leader would be oozing out along the stone sluice prepared to receive it before he could get there and prevent it.

So, two paces off, he took quick aim, and hurled his long sword as if it were a lance. It hurtled, sizzling, through the bright sunshine, caught the knife-wielding right arm of Pocapa Tlal across the wrist, and broke bones.

A moment later and Eric leaped on the sacred form of the high priest, thrust under him one gaunt knee, gave him a mighty shove and propelled him headlong down the steps. With the same movement he recovered the sharp sacrificial knife where it had fallen on the platform, and severed the rawhide thongs which were already beginning to force the ebbing life from Eric's chief.

While the puma soldiers were running up from below, their lances poised, shouting a babel of quacking imprecations, Rorek's chief archer gently but swiftly lifted him to his feet.

With one glance the red-haired leader took in the desperate situation. He saw the great plaza a welter of conflicting purposes. Puma skins were fighting the wearers of the jaguar. Many of them did not know what it was all about, and evidently thought the long-awaited conflict between Za Ramna and Pocapa Tlal had been precipitated.

Others—scores in number—were fighting back against the fierce onslaught of the archers. The five had kept their formation and their sense of direction. They had seen the objective of Eric, and fought to protect him in his errand of rescue. They stood, part way up the steps, fighting back the onrushing horde.

Eric recovered his sword, and at the same moment Rorek picked up the fallen knife of the high priest. It would be a scant weapon, but better than nothing. He remembered where he had left his own buckler, bow, arrows and sword the night before when entering the rear door of the temple to see Za Chel—in a thicket of bamboo not far away. Could he reach it now?

Calling to Eric to bring the archers up the steps and then down to the rear, Rorek began at once to execute a plan he had quickly formed. It had a double object—to get his weapons and to rescue Za Chel. He intended to take her from the temple and to carry her with him into the country far from this hideous Uxmal.

With this thought, armed only with the Mayan knife, Rorek leaped up the steps. As he gained the top, he met the forefront of the puma guard coming from the rear to see what it was all about. They carried their stone-tipped lances half-heartedly.

WITH A WILD shout he sprang on them—one man against fifty. But what a man—tall, flaming-haired, desperate. If even one had held his lance stoutly, he might have stopped the Norseman's onrush. But they huddled like sheep, and he dashed into them, cutting, one down through the neck, another up into the heart, a third straight in the face, and, as these three fell, the others huddled back. He leaped through them, to the front door of the temple. He banged against it.

The door was closed. Rorek wasted no time, but dashed along the platform and around the temple. More puma-clad soldiers were coming up the rear steps. Ignorant of what had happened, they fell to right and left as the man they thought was on the sacrificial stone charged madly through, calling, as he went, "Eric! This way!"

Down the rear steps Rorek plunged. Yes. There, not fifty feet beyond the last steps, lay the clump of bamboo. He reached it unscathed, and with vast relief found his buck-

ler shield, his bow and arrows, and long sword where he
had laid them.

In a moment he was armored, and turned to face his foes.
They were gathering swiftly now—in hundreds, as they
followed the fighting archers, who were obeying the orders
given in the plaza, to fight only with lances and swords.

Half of his object achieved, Rorek breathed freely for a
moment, though the more important half was not accomplished. He must rescue Za Chel.

There, fifty feet away, lay the door through which he had
gained access to her the night before and thus precipitated
this crisis. He must go that way again.

In the space between, the archers were fighting, each
surrounded by many foes, but the Mayans fought without
head. Most of them attacked without reference to each
other, and few indeed but wrought more havoc on their
own fellows than on the Norsemen.

Rorek shoved and slashed a way through to the lower
door of the temple, and there he clamored loudly, finding
it locked, but to no avail. There was no response.

Za Chel was imprisoned somewhere in that huge pile of
masonry. He cried aloud, but no answer came to his eager
call. Finally, as a dozen of the jaguar-skins came around
the corner and dashed at him with their lances, he found
he had enough to do to parry with his heavy buckler.

He would have to cut his way out of this, and save
himself and his archers. They had accounted for perhaps
fifty of the Mayans without losing more than a little blood;
but what were fifty in such an army? It only maddened the
others and drove them on, though many refused to enter
the lists with beings they feared might be gods.

Rorek rushed back to Eric, whom he found flanked by Olav and Hemnet, and back to back with them the trio of Galko, Donal and Wolfkin.

"Archers!" he cried.

"Hai, Rorek!"

"Cut your way straight through yon street, and on through the town."

"Aye, Rorek!"

In a moment they had formed the Norse phalanx, shield to shield, making a solid wall of armor, from their necks to their shins, and slowly began to force a way in a direction opposite from the Yellow Palace where the emperor even now was in startled conference with Pocapa Tlal, as the high priest nursed his broken arm.

The stone-tipped lances made little effect upon the shields, but, as the distance between the Norsemen and the Mayans increased, one of the Mayan captains, more resourceful than the others, thought it about time to use arrows. He gave orders to his men to fall back, form ranks for shooting and to fire.

In a moment twenty arrows clattered against the shields, or flew harmlessly over the Norse heads.

"Halt!" said Rorek. "Fill your bows! We will show them what shooting is!"

And they did. The seven fired as one—and without a miss. Seven Mayans fell—and the foremost of them was the audacious captain. The others broke and fled.

"Good!" said Rorek. "Now we can depart in peace!"

Eric halted him. "Wait!" he said. "Wolfkin is injured."

Rorek examined the smallest of his archers, the one who stood no more than five feet eight inches high. A Mayan arrow had penetrated his breast. It seemed only a flesh wound, but, as he placed his fingers on it, he suddenly stiffened, shrieked in agony, and in a moment was dead.

Eric pulled out the arrow. It had gone in only a little.

"Poisoned!" said Rorek.

"We had better leave him and hasten on," suggested Eric.

"No!" Rorek replied. "Lift him up and bring him with us. When we are safely alone we will give him proper Norse burial. No Mayan must ever know he has been killed."

14

A DREAM OF EMPIRE

THE NORSEMEN FLED toward the west, for the great temple at Uxmal faced the east, and they had fought around to its rear and escaped that way. Their progress was somewhat impeded by the body of Wolfkin; but their mighty sinews drove swiftly westward.

The city extended for more than three miles in all directions, but as they went on they found the streets more and more deserted, for most of the people had crowded up to the plaza to witness the sacrifice. The few they saw fled before they could approach, for the news of the miraculous rescue of the giant red-haired stranger who had been the guest of the emperor, and whom Pocapa Tlal had marked for sacrifice to Ah Bolan Dzacab, spread far more quickly than the Norse archers could run.

Back on the steps of the Yellow Palace, Pocapa Tlal had given his orders to slay the strangers, but, when his puma-clad soldiers had done their best, had let fly their poisoned arrows without avail, and then had been met by instant death for seven of their number in the form of seven long arrows, the survivors had come back to report their repulse and their fear of these tall gods.

Angrily Za Ramna ordered his jaguar soldiers to go forth

and apprehend the villainous strangers. They obeyed, but not with any too great alacrity, and their captains saw to it that they did not encounter the godlike ones too suddenly. Half the afternoon was gone, and Rorek, with his band, had reached safely the very fringe of Uxmal.

Pocapa Tlal's puma soldiers discreetly remained with the high priest. He did not feel any too secure, after what had happened. Besides, was it not the business of the emperor to catch this renegade, this impudent "sacrifice" who had had the temerity to escape from under the very edge of the holy knife? So he kept his guards close about him, as insurance against what might come, while he proceeded by fulminations to arouse the half-hearted Za Ramna to a furious but futile realization of how atrociously his hospitality had been abused.

The captain-general of the jaguar-skin army led the way, asking the skulking inhabitants of the low huts—the mice-minded, weak-willed Mayans—which way the strangers had gone. He found only dull stupidity, frightened ignorance; he was told of flaxen and red-haired gods taking wings, or disappearing in a burst of lightning.

Whereupon he called a council of war with his officers. After long debate, they decided that the Norsemen would surely try to get back to the coast whence they had come, to reach the boat, which was beached on the sands, and so elude pursuit.

The captain-general gave orders to his army to about-face toward the east and apprehend the marauders there, before they could reach the coast and gain the refuge of their fabulous boat.

At about the same time, in the bed of a rocky declivity,

just beyond the city, Rorek and the five survivors rested under an overhanging cliff, at the edge of the jungle.

Wolfkin's body lay near, and the six sat on their haunches in close discussion.

"We can skirt the edge of the city and so beat back to that long road whence we came," said Eric.

"Why?" asked Rorek, simply.

"To reach our boat—"

"And what then?"

"Then we will be safe."

"Safe for what?"

"To regain the sea, our only friend."

ROREK REPLIED CALMLY, "You call the sea our friend, when it has robbed us of our homes and of all our comrades?"

"It did not rob us of Wolfkin," Olav muttered.

"Aye!" solemnly assented Rorek. "We paid one—but one only to defeat the Mayans!"

"Defeat!" exclaimed Hemnet in surprise. "You call this sorry flight a victory?"

"What else?" Rorek looked calmly from one to another.

It was indeed surprising to them. They had fought with fury, willing to die if need be, but now when the berserk rage had gone, when the excitement of the contest was a matter only of memory, they looked upon themselves as refugee sailors, separated from their sole home, and surrounded by myriad enemies. They expressed this to him, in their own way, one by one. It seemed to them so logical; so inevitable.

Rorek listened gravely and then said proudly:

"We are victors! We have made the greatest foray

known to any Viking—greater even than the foray of King
Gunneborn into the land of the Franks. We have sighted a
land greater than Wolf the Crow sighted west of Iceland.
We have before us a vaster plunder than was taken from the
Scots by Sauer the Great. Would you abandon this when
it is half plucked?"

This was most astounding. The mouths of the five were
open. They loved Rorek; they adored him; but some of
them wondered, without giving voice to their fears, if those
long hours in the sun on that fierce stone, with the rawhide
biting his flesh, had not, perhaps, cracked his wit—just a
bit.

Donal, the Hibernian, who did not relish any reference
to the Vikings' plucking of the Scots, voiced the common
doubt.

"You say we have half-plucked this plunder, Rorek?"

"Aye!"

Donal held forth his bare hands, where the blood was
drying from the scratches that had come as he hacked his
way through the lances of the puma soldiers.

"Where is any plunder, my chief?" he asked simply.

"You see it not?" Rorek insisted.

Galko—dull-witted Galko—loyal, yet stupid—
mumbled:

"Nay, Rorek—I see we have only bruises and hunger—
and Wolfkin dead and unburied."

Rorek laid an affectionate palm on the arm of the
staunch, unseeing Galko. "Have patience," he said.

Then he included all as he went on: "I have studied
these Mayans. I have asked about their past. They are not
like us. They have never been in real danger from outside.

They are not fighting men, despite their ridiculous armies. And already they are whipped—in their own minds. They believe us gods. And they will never believe anything else. Not the rulers, but the people. And so we will bide our time; and when the time is ripe take what is our due. Now, do you understand why I ask you to have patience?"

Galko slowly shook his head. His stout body would follow where his leader led, but in the mind he faltered. Rorek's scheme was too exalted.

Donal, Olav and Hemnet were equally unseeing. They all strongly counseled getting back to the ship and escaping by sea from this alarming land. They were inclined to blame Rorek for not having seized what they could from Taycapin when they first saw her, and getting off with so much. For now, what had they?

Eric was silent. He felt with the men, but he would say nothing to embarrass his chief.

THEN ROREK TOOK their minds from their immediate problem by ordering the burial of Wolfkin. The favored Norse burial—at sea—was impossible. The alternative as known to the Vikings they quickly arranged. They wound the body in huge plantain leaves, lacking cloth, and tied it up with creeper from the jungle, laying Wolfkin's sword by his side, close to his hand, for use when he reached Valhalla; then they hoisted it to the fork of the nearest tree and tied it there—so the air might the more easily penetrate its mortal part and the more easily separate therefrom the immortal.

They bowed their heads while Rorek repeated the invocation to Thor to accept the valorous spirit of his chosen warrior who had expired properly, with his face to his enemies, and while taking with him as servants, the spirits of many who fought against him.

It was now nearly dusk, and they had rested.

We will go on," Rorek announced. "We can travel best by night, for no Mayan travels by night and all live together, in the towns and cities. Thus we will be unmolested."

"Which way, O Chief?" asked Eric, as he prepared to lead the five.

Rorek pointed west.

"But our ship lies east!"

"If there were no other reason to avoid that," Rorek softly replied, "we must keep away from it now because it is there they will search for us."

"But if we have conquered them—" Hemnet objected.

"Ah!" Rorek laughed subtly. "They do not know as yet."

"I guess not," Galko grumbled, "and when shall we tell them?"

"When we can force them to surrender their land to us and become our slaves!" He owed Za Ramna no debt of hospitality now, after this!

In the suffusing saffron of the setting sun Rorek's face took on a look of unearthly radiance—of some high purpose. That his thoughts were back there with Za Chel in the prison she called a temple, his men could not know. They saw only the stern resolve of their beloved chief, they felt only the vast self-confidence of one who had never failed them.

"Where, then, do we go?" the dutiful Eric asked.

"West—to the hills."

"The hills?"

"Aye! To the land of the Olmecas!"

"Who?" they demanded in chorus, alive with almost childish curiosity now. "Who are the Olmecas?"

"They will be, I hope, our friends. At least, we will endeavor to make them our friends."

So the march west to the hills began, in the swift tropic twilight. As they marched, from one to the other they repeated wonderingly the word, "Olmecas!"

Finally Donal, the inquisitive, could endure no more. He plucked Rorek by the tunic as he strode ahead. "O Chief," he called, "be patient with our ignorance."

"You are not ignorant, Donal!" replied Rorek. "Remember that, to a Mayan, you are as a god."

"Then tell me why we seek the Olmecas."

"They have numbers, and shall become our allies, and with numbers we can return and prove our fiefship over Maya!"

Whereupon peace settled on the marching Norsemen as they went farther inland—still more abandoning their traditional mother, the sea. Rorek was no man to be bound by tradition.

15

THE MOUNTAIN PASS

THE ROADS IN Mayaland were never very worn, for they never existed more than a few years. Though living solely by agriculture, the people did not know the use of the plow. They used the land as long as it would produce for them their maize, squash, beans and the like, and then abandoned it. They got new land by cutting down new jungle and letting the old worn land go back to jungle. Land would thus produce profitably six, eight—at most a dozen years.

The people never lived in single families, but always in towns and cities—a gregarious, communal life. When they abandoned the old land they abandoned the old towns— made of palm frond thatches thrown across untrimmed poles. At the same time they abandoned the old roads, which, in a short time, the jungle swallowed again.

Knowing this, having thought upon it, Rorek shrewdly sought a course to the west that would elude the jaguar soldiers of Za Ramna. He felt sure they would proceed along the new, used roads, and would look for the fugitives among the habitations of the wayside.

Therefore, Rorek avoided the new roads and took only those which bore no signs of having been traversed for several years. He saw no one, and none saw him, or his devoted five.

They lived on the fruits—on bananas, coconuts, pineapples and persimmons, though the season was too young yet for the latter to be fully ripe.

A little to the north was the city of Kabah; a little to the south the city of Labna. Between spread a patch of new jungle; with an old road, already infested with creepers. There Rorek and his archers went, while ten miles away, on the new road, a detachment of jaguar soldiers bravely marched, four abreast.

When the outlying Mayans finally heard about it, they attributed marvelous ingenuity to the divine intelligence of the godlike stranger, and the omniscient wisdom within his red head. The incident was one of many which served to build up his legend and to render him a character of mythical repute.

Two days later Rorek avoided Hockob, another city of the plain, in the same manner. Then he bore south and far to the west of Bacalar, which was the outmost of the chief cities of Mayaland toward the interior.

Beyond Bacalar came the mountains, and beyond the mountains dwelt the Olmecas.

On the seventh day, in the early dawn, before they started again on the trail, which had now reached the foothills, Rorek said to the men: "From now we will climb. The soldiers will come no further, for the mountains are the natural barriers of Mayaland."

They grunted a pleased response, though why they should care about the soldiers was not clear. They had not been molested since leaving Uxmal. Rorek had steered them clear of mishap, and already their buoyant spirits had recovered.

They never asked how he knew what he told them. It never occurred to them as worthy of comment that he, a stranger like themselves, could tell them the intricacies of this new land, and be able to find his way about in it more deftly than did its inhabitants. To them that was a natural attribute of Rorek, their chief. In their way they worshipped him as did those Mayans who knew him even less well.

IN THE FOOTHILLS the jungle became denser. Hence, the Norsemen were obliged to go more slowly, for the roads were indistinct paths, made by beasts and used infrequently by man.

The bright colors everywhere delighted the Norsemen, used to somber grays and blacks. Often, as they pushed into a thicket, a fierce chattering would ensue where they had disturbed the roosting place of a flock of macaws, and the gorgeous birds, in their orange, blue, and scarlet, would fill the air with plumage as they flew off in interminable pairs—hundreds, thousands. They had given up shooting macaws and parrakeets, for they were tough eating.

Their second day in the foothills they killed three peccaries and stopped a day to show how well they had learned the Mayan feasting habit. The savory pig flesh thus steamed in plantain leaves furnished the meat for which they had been longing.

The way grew steeper and slower. Ravines that looked impassable loomed ahead, and they managed to get through only because Rorek insisted that here was the way. For days they had seen no sign of human beings.

Finally, above them, thousands of feet it seemed, the path led through a cave and under a ledge of rock. They could just see daylight beyond.

"There?" said Rorek. "I recognize it. The Pass of Tikal!"

"How can you recognize it?" demanded Eric. "Were you here before, pray?"

"I recognize it from the description of Za Ramna. The Pass of Tikal is the extreme western gate of Mayaland. Beyond are the Olmecas. There is no reason for the Mayans to go beyond the mountains, for over there are only more passes and high jungle, and the Mayans cannot find any land to cultivate, but when they try to go the Olmecas will not let them. Down here in the lowland, in the level country, is the place for Mayans. Up there, in the sky, with the llamas, is the land of the Olmecas. Come."

Stoutly he led the way, but it was an all-day job to reach even the lower ledge of the cave. The sun was going down as they got there, and they camped for the night.

Early the next morning they prepared to go through the Pass of Tikal. Eric strode on, in advance, though he was breathing hard, because of the altitude. They were fully a mile above the level of the sea.

He was eager to get through that hole in the cave and see what was on the other side. For a moment he was lost to the sight of the others, who were more bothered by the altitude and were obliged to go more slowly.

Suddenly they were startled by an angry shout from Eric, and in a moment he was back among them, holding his face in his hand. In the other was a little round pellet, the size of a hen's egg.

"What is it, Eric?" they demanded, crowding about him.

He revealed his face. A welt was red on his cheek bone. "This," he held out the pellet, "was thrown at me by some one beyond the pass."

"It is a black stone!" said Donal.

"No," said Rorek, taking it and examining it, "it is an *olli*."

He showed it to them, and thrust his thumb nail into one side, where it gave. He passed it about. They all felt the pellet wonderingly. It was not a stone, for all its hardness, for it gave on any side where it was pressed.

Rorek took it, threw it on the rocky floor of the path. It bounced, and he caught the rubber ball. "That is what Za Ramna told me," he said; "it is the greeting of the Olmeca."

"A rude greeting!" Eric grumbled, rubbing his cheek.

"This," Rorek went on, handling the piece of hard substance, "is a stuff they take from trees. They call it *olli*, and they take their name from it—the Olmecas. It is the only land in the world where they make stones from the gum of trees. Come, I wish to know more about it. If what Za Ramna tells me is true, this *olli* would be capital stuff with which to calk the seams in a boat."

Rorek pushed on.

"BEWARE!" ERIC CRIED; "an *olli* in the eye would not be so pleasant."

But the chief went forth with a shout, his arm thrust far before him, and crying in Mayan, "Greetings to the Olmeca!"

The others held back. Eric's reception had not been any too encouraging. Peering around a bowlder, they saw, to them, a very strange sight.

A swarthy stout figure, in a close cape of some skin, appeared at the head of the pass. They could see only his upper body. He watched a minute the approaching Rorek. Then he took from a pocket at his side another pellet and threw it swiftly at the Norse chief.

Instead of dodging, Rorek reached out with his hand and deftly caught the pellet.

With that the man in the cape spoke to another, as yet unseen, and a second figure appeared. The two came clearly into view. They were sturdy men, a little larger in figure and taller than the average Mayan.

They stood stockily at the head of the pass, blocking the way, as Rorek approached.

Finally the archers saw Rorek bow to the two, who formally returned the bow. Then the three stood for a long time, silhouetted against the daylight beyond the pass.

After that Rorek turned and beckoned to his archers to come on.

So the Norsemen went through the Pass of Tikal into the land of the Olmecas, and gasped at the beauty they saw. For tumbling out of the pass at their very feet fell a roaring river, cascading below into a gorgeous valley. The river flowed west to the Pacific, as yet unknown to white men, for the Olmecas dwelt along the peninsula divide.

A condor soared lazily in the far blue, and below, far down, they saw flocks of llamas grazing in a fertile valley which seemed up-ended, so steep were its sides. Yet so luscious was its greenery that the llamas stood thigh-deep in the tall grass.

The Olmecan guides led them on until, turning a rock in the path, they came suddenly to a thatched village. It was composed of a dozen huts sprawling in a little coulee on the mountain side. It was too high for palms. The thatches were made of slabs of cedar, long shingles that grouped themselves in pretty patterns and hung down low over the doorways. For the nights were cool.

In the open space before the huts two grown boys, perhaps twelve years old, were batting across a lattice work one of the queer bounding pellets of *olli*. One would hit the ground with it, and it would fly up to the hand of the other and he would return it, and so on, until one missed, to the accompaniment of peals of delight from the near-by spectators.

The foremost scout apologized to Rorek. "That is not the sacred game of *olli* played by the priests on feast days," he explained. "That would not be right for us poor mountaineers to do. It is only the boys, who would thus practice to grow up and be good priests."

As they rested, Rorek and his archers learned that among the Olmecas proficiency with the *olli* pellet in the national game of driving it back and forth across a low wall was considered one of the chief male accomplishments.

Here, in the rare air, seemed a pleasant place for sojourn.

16

A LEGENDARY HERO

FROM MAYAPAN, POCAPA Tlal mended his fences nicely. While the jaguar soldiers of the emperor were ramping about the countryside to the east, and a small contingent proceeded even along the roads to the west for surety, Pocapa Tlal sent his most trusted captain with a company of puma soldiers, under guidance of the peccary scout of the Princess Taycapin who had first seen the Norse boat, direct to the far eastern shore, beyond the jungle, where the fairhaired strangers had been perceived rising from the foam.

There they found the Vikings' ship, with its swan-like throat, and its devilishly long oars—fit vessel for the wafting of a god out of the great waters; and they proceeded to obey the orders of the high priest. Though not without fear and trepidation.

It took a brave Mayan to raise his stone hatchet and bring it down with destructive force on that vessel of the gods. But there were no gods visible and the orders of Pocapa Tlal, who was very near the gods, as all knew, were imperative.

After one blow had broken the nearest oar, and no dire result had occurred, the other puma-clad worthies took heart. They leaped in valiantly to the attack, and in short order had entirely destroyed the lovely vessel which had accomplished the perilous voyage from far-off Greenland.

They piled the wreckage up on the shore and placed under it burning charcoal carried for the purpose, while three of Pocapa Tlal's assistants intoned the celebration of the sacrifice to the outraged Ah Bolan Dzacab.

The contingent of puma-clad soldiers, accompanied by drums and flageolets, danced about the ashes and charred embers, far into the night.

"To thee, Ah Bolan Dzacab, mightiest of the mighty, we offer the bones and lives and hopes of the devils who came to Maya masquerading in the forms of gods!" intoned the priests.

"Aie! Aie!" wailed the puma soldiers.

The next day they started back to Mayapan, though ahead of them the conch telegraph had carried the welcome news to the wily ears of the high priest, who sent on to Uxmal his personal messenger with the good news to Za Ramna.

As the news spread and grew through the cities— through Ixaisal and Hockob, through Uxmal and Mayapan, through Bacalar and Labna, and a dozen others—it lost nothing in the telling.

In short, it became a national celebration of the rescue of Maya from the menace of the terrible blond strangers. They were gone. The vessel in which they came was only of wood and had been destroyed like any other vessel of wood. And who could say they were not destroyed in their vessel?

That Rorek and his archers were destroyed, that they had been burned in the fire which had consumed their ship on the far sands, was soon almost universally believed. Almost! Save among some poor lowly field workers who longed to dream—merely dream—of a triumph of other gods over the lords who rode their backs.

IN THIS FORM the news reached the great temple at Uxmal, and was told to Za Chel. Her white god, with the hair of flaming red, had been consumed in fire by the soldiers of Pocapa Tlal. Praise be to Ah Bolan Dzacab!

She could not doubt that it was a wonderful blessing to Maya, that it would serve to propitiate Ah Bolan Dzacab, and induce him to wring his vast eyes and pour upon the fields those copious tears of gladness which alone could bring the land plenty.

From her earliest infancy Za Chel had been trained to believe that nothing more desirable could happen to a maiden of Maya than to be chosen as the bride of the Sun. This far exceeded any mortal joy of mating with a mere man.

In her tenth year, she had been consecrated to the temple with an accompanying display of flowers. The feast and dancing, which had lasted far into the night, had filled her with pride and exultant happiness.

Then, in her twelfth year, when it was seen how Nature had marked her as a queen in bearing, and when the high priest himself, after due survey and deliberation, had announced that she, and she alone, was the fairest daughter of Maya, and she had been anointed with the sacred oil of cassia, and given her own special tirewomen and the sacred inner apartments of the great temple for a domicile, it had seemed her joy must be complete.

After that, as the First Virgin of the Sun, she took precedence over all in the land, save only her father, Za Ramna, the emperor, and Pocapa Tlal, the high priest. Even the Princess Taycapin, with her shrewd hard eyes, was obliged to come behind her in the annual state processions to the ancient capital at Chichen Itza.

Some day, she knew, she would achieve the highest honor reserved for a daughter of Maya—to be offered as the living bride to the all-consuming Sun God, who, in return, would command Ah Bolan Dzacab, the long-nosed God of Rain, to give more plentifully of his stores to the people of Maya.

Her body and her soul would be merged immortally with the Sun God. Meanwhile, to him alone must her thoughts be directed.

Dutifully she did so direct her thoughts—mostly. Yet there was the memory of that day above the sacrificial stone when she had gazed into the blue eyes of the prostrate stranger.

Something beyond herself had caused her to murmur to him that in the after life her spirit would find his. How could she have uttered such a thought? It was strangely perverse, so contrary to the training of the priests, and the admonitions of her father. She tried to put aside the memory of this dereliction.

In the day it was not so hard to forget those blue eyes, and that red hair—how the flash of that red hair persisted in her mind's eye! But after the Sun was gone—the god to whom she was promised—she thought there could be no harm in remembering those fair features.

He had given her one swift glance of appeal, which had so plainly said that she alone could save him—from what?

Surely not from the sacrifice, for that was only an honor! But the appeal—the mere memory of that glance—stirred some inner depths in her which came to mean more than all the teaching of her short life, more than all the words of the constant priests.

Was she disloyal to her bridegroom that was to be—the Sun God? In the day she feared it, but each night, again, her mind reached avidly for that mellow memory, and she never failed to fall asleep gazing wistfully into those appealing, yet strong eyes. Never before had she seen blue eyes. And in a man!

Nay! He must have been a god!

17

DOOMED

AS THE WEEKS slid into the heat of summer, and Maya, below on the fertile plains of the peninsula, sweltered in the ever-increasing glow of the molten sun, Rorek and his archers grew more and more entranced with the pleasures of their life in the land of the Olmecas.

There it was never hot. The lowest of the valleys was a mile above the sea, and the upper ones stuck into the sky fully two miles. It was said that far up near the peak of Orizaba, the great mountain which could be seen on clear days, lived people who never dared come down because their ears would burst and they would bleed to death. The Olmecans never climbed that far. Hardy though they were, their breath failed them when they went above the two-mile height.

Up there in the land of the sky the Olmecans paid no heed to the infernal whims of Ah Bolan Dzacab, the Long-nosed God of Rain, who filled so much of the lives and thoughts of the lowly Mayans. It was not necessary to pray to him nor to propitiate him, for not in the memory of any Olmecan, nor in the legend of any Olmecan, had rain ever failed them.

The rain came almost every day in the year, an hour or

two before midday. If it missed one day it invariably came the next, and it did not miss more than ten times a year. And the sky always cleared in the afternoon.

If it had not been for the providential *olli* there would have been too much rain. The houses and the capes of llama and goat skin would not have held against it, but the *olli* taken from the trees, whence it flowed in slow drops when properly cut, could be stuffed into the cracks and held along the seams of the skins, and thus the rain could be charmed away.

No wonder the Olmecans believed they were the most favored people on earth. They had all the rain they could use, and more, with means to control the superabundance. They were never hot, and never too cold, though it was chilly up there at night.

Better than all else, they were not obliged to live entirely on the meager grasses from the fields like those wretched Mayans on the plains below. There was plenty of wild game: peccaries and pheasants, and quail, with an occasional puma. Sometimes they feasted on baked rattlesnake, a delicacy.

They were not obliged to give thought to overpopulation as did the rulers of Maya where children thrived, for in the mountains, with the daily changes from heat to cold, and the constant rains, most of the children died before they could be inured to the climate. Only one in four or five lived.

But the survivor—Ah! He was an Olmecan, a true man of rubber, hardy, worth any dozen Mayans.

Rorek and his archers thrived there in great shape. After they were acclimated, and could exercise without stopping to gain breath, because of the rarefied atmosphere, they came into a joyous existence.

If a Norseman was to live in the tropics the land of the Olmecas was the land for him. The vegetarianism of the Mayans had palled on them. Here they reverted to their natural meat-eating instinct. Hunting up and down the hills or through the valleys and ravines, strengthened and toughened them. They became wiry, alert, farsighted, adept in all the ways of the mountaineers.

The Norse archery at once placed them high in Olmecan estimation, for they could shoot almost twice as far as any native. Rorek especially, with his sharpshooter's eye, never missed. Once he shot out of a condor's mouth, across a valley, a baby llama which the bird was stealing—by slitting the lower bill of the huge flapping bird. The little llama ran back to its mother, unharmed.

There was no Olmecan who did not honor him. They called him *Tolteca*—Great Survivor—for he had not claimed any supernatural powers, and had frankly told them his origin, and whence he had come with his archers—and they marveled at his exploits in Maya.

Rorek found that these mountaineers had no recognized chief. Each little village had a sort of headman, but he was without either duties or powers. They were individuals, each content with his freedom and the largesse nature had provided. Thievery was unknown.

As the months passed, however, the Olmecans came to look upon Rorek with great respect, as their strongest and wisest man. But that was all, among that independent people.

FIVE MAYAN MONTHS of twenty days each elapsed after

Rorek and his archers had escaped from Uxmal. In their rainy cloudland they were not conscious of lack of food or the means to secure it.

But one day the lookout from the Pass of Tikal came with tidings from the plains of Maya. It was the month of Mac—the pestle—when the maize should be ripe for cutting; the time of harvest.

Yet the maize was sullen in the stalk, down in the lowlands. The ears were blighted. Maya was threatened with famine, for the rains had not come. Ah Bolan Dzacab had frowned on Maya. The Rain God was displeased.

"What will they do?" asked Rorek of the lookout.

"They will offer the usual sacrifice to Ah Bolan Dzacab," casually replied the indifferent lookout.

An evil premonition seized Rorek.

"What sacrifice?" he asked.

"Of a virgin. Those poor devils who have no rain!"

"When?"

The Olmecan lookout was surprised at the interest displayed by the great red-crowned Toltec. "I have talked with a Mayan, who says the sacrifice has been announced to occur at Chichen Itza on the last day of the month of Mac. They will offer a virgin to the Sun God so that he may command Ah Bolan Dzacab to give rain—else Maya is destroyed."

Rorek felt his heart almost stop beating as he asked, "And the name of this virgin—did you learn her name?"

"Za something. The Mayan says she is the daughter of the emperor, Za Ramna—and a sweet morsel!"

Za Chel! Why had thought of her pressed on him so distinctly these last few nights after the sun went down?

Not a day since he left Uxmal had he failed to think of her, but of late—after sundown—she seemed enveloping him with an appeal so poignant he had been tempted to steal away from his archers and his devoted Olmecans and to strive to see her once more in the hidden place in the great temple—if so difficult a thing were possible.

She had saved him—without doubt—by relaying that one word *"Ska-na"* to Eric that day on the temple steps. Did he not owe her something now?

A mighty passion seemed to seize him. His great hands clenched as he knew he would risk anything to save her—from herself, from those bloodthirsty fanatic millions. But how?

18

THE WELL OF SACRIFICE

A LONG AND colorful procession turned at the crossroads half-way from Uxmal to Mayapan, and headed toward Chichen Itza. At its head rode the emperor in his state litter, above which floated the long red banner denoting the day of sacrifice, which had arrived.

For that day all labor throughout Maya had ceased. The wilting maize stood untended. The half-nourished vegetables lay unwatched on the ground.

For to-day Ah Bolan Dzacab would be invoked. The Chief Virgin would become the Bride of the Sun in the great well at Chichen Itza. And the crops would be saved.

Meanwhile the populace would watch and pray—and feast on what little there was left.

At the crossroads stood the squat, morose figure of the High Priest. He dipped his obsidian manikin of temporal power as the emperor passed, and fell in behind him, with his puma-clad soldiers, as they turned toward Chichen Itza.

A long space was left—fully a thousand yards where no person dared enter the road. Then, alone, head erect, eyes on high, rode the Sun Virgin; alone, on the sacred llama.

For once, on her breast, hung the great emerald of

Cochibar, the most precious jewel in the empire. The emperor had loaned it to her—for the early part of the day only. Before she became the Sun's bride she would return it, for when she joined the god she would have no need of jewels. Za Chel herself would be the jewel of Maya in the bosom of the god, even as the emerald of Cochibar lay now on her fair breast.

The flageolets droned; the drums beat a somber, monotonous, dull rhythm. *Boom! Boom!*

The Mayans fell down on their faces as she passed. So bright was the beautified countenance of the Bride of the Sun that they dared see it only askance and then in holy wonder. It gave them a quick catch at the heart to know that before the evening came that lovely apparition, fairest maiden in Maya, would be forever dimmed in the dark well beside the ruins of the old stone temple in the ancient capital.

Za Ramna rode on, twisting and turning along the narrow road, one of the oldest in the empire, threading a solemn passage between the burned-out maize stalks.

Morosely his jaguar-clad soldiers, with reversed lances, inclosed him, front and rear. Pocapa Tlal, surrounded by his puma skins, was swept along in his litter of scented rosewood with its covering of saffron cotton.

Then came Za Chel, the beautiful hummingbird-feathered *huitzin* still flowing across her body—a few hours more and it would be taken from her forever—and the great emerald snug in its green fire atop her velvety breast. Behind her trooped the forty wives of Za Ramna, heads hanging down, feet rubbed in ashes, for none of them had

She took a last look in the mica mirror at the
loveliness soon to be offered to the Sun God.

been fortunate enough to provide for Maya a male heir to the throne.

And then Taycapin—withdrawn from sight in her litter with its purple covers, and accompanied by her cotton-quilted warriors, carrying their bows upside down and their lances uncapped, for the day was not military but religious.

The road wound through the new jungle, among the lands abandoned as useless only the decade before. Here already the lush creeper and the stout greasewood were clogging the drifted furrows.

They came to the Ravine of the Ants, where the burrowing insects had destroyed all vegetation, and had piled high in all directions their enormous hills, thriving, it seemed, on the disaster to the woodland and the fecund earth.

The emperor shuddered; the High Priest shuddered; the soldiers looked to neither right nor left. For it seemed as if this Ravine of the Ants symbolized the future of Maya. Squirming masses of insects crawling over each other, devouring each other, building huge houses in which they could only breed and perish.

Only Za Chel looked on high and was radiant.

OUT OF THE Ravine of the Ants the procession climbed as hastily as possible and entered then the final winding road through the last mesa that led to the sacred center of empire. Up they went for a few miles, and suddenly there was a break through a cliff, and there—below—lay Chichen Itza.

Down they went into the city founded by the father of the race, Ra-Mu. They passed the Hall of the Jaguars, where the jungle creepers were curling about the toes of the black and yellow stone beasts that formed the entrance columns.

Many shuddered near the Palace of the Snake, where the columns in the form of rattlesnakes, made of porphyry inlaid with shell, were so realistic that later in the day those who imbibed *mishla* too freely would imagine the rattles sounding and the stone snakes about to strike.

At length they reached the Yellow Temple of the Sun— the great masterpiece of Mayan architecture, with its front inlaid with a mosaic of jet and shell, chalcedony and obsidian. And there, to the right, lay the well—the Well of the Virgins!

A yawning black pit no more than twelve feet across the top, with vines straggling down. It was bottomless—so the Mayans believed. At least from its depths no one ever returned. Did it contain water?

Who knew?

Nests of vipers were concealed in the vines that clung to its sides, and the priests fed them mice and rabbits to encourage them to cling there.

Into the well the Brides of the Sun were dropped, gently but firmly, by the officiating priests on the days of sacrifice. None had ever returned, though often their shrieks had lasted far into the night of the day of the sacrifice. The shrieks were, of course, the evil demons within them being exorcised by Ah Bolan Dzacab before they could be received, purified, by the august Sun God in person.

For a thousand years the plaza of Chichen Itza had lasted—for a thousand years the red and yellow and black and purple stones had reared their beautiful man-made fronts to the tropic sun in that fair rectangle.

But for five hundred years the city which surrounded the beautiful plaza with its temples and palaces had been wasting away. Once the chief city of Maya, it was now no more than a relic, for the land surrounding it, from which the people lived, had wasted away and had reverted to jungle.

Even now, before a sacrifice, like as not, a python would have to be driven from a resting place in the Temple of the Sun by the officiating priests before the Sun's bride could be prepared. The heat that came from the large stones was favored by pythons—and lizards. Chichen Itza was only a ruin—yet a sacred shrine. Here, and here only, in the great Well of the Virgins, the crops of Maya could be saved. Here, and here only, Ah Bolan Dzacab would listen to his august master, the Sun God.

Here, and here only, could the national sacrifice be properly offered—for here lay the well. The dread, the inspired, the sacred Well of Chichen Itza.

ZA RAMNA SOLEMNLY crossed the plaza to the droning of the drums and the whining of the flageolets, ascended the long steps of the Red Palace, and placed himself on the prepared dais of red porphyry, whence he could look across to the well. And see his daughter dropped to the vipers! He was pale as he majestically took his seat.

The jaguar soldiers of the emperor properly lined the plaza to prevent the crowds, which even now were swarming along the roads through the Ravine of the Ants, from coming too near the mouth of the well.

Then through the opening toward the road came the High Priest's puma soldiers. Rather pettishly they shoved the nearest jaguar skins aside, for this was a religious day, not a temporal one, and a jaguar skin was subordinate to a puma for this once. The captain called stertorously:

"Way! Way for His Excellency the High Priest! Way for Pocapa Tlal, the mouthpiece of the gods!"

Pocapa Tlal thereupon dismounted from his litter, at the entrance to the plaza, seized firmly his new and stout manikin of black obsidian, held it aloft threateningly, as if to assure all of its omnipotence, and strode magnificently toward the Temple of the Sun.

His assistants had preceded him by the better part of an hour and had been busily engaged driving the sleeping reptiles from all the vantage spots, whence one or more might impertinently drop during the proceedings and perhaps disturb an apostrophe of the mouthpiece of the gods.

Thus Pocapa Tlal strode confidently into the great temple, blessed by a thousand years of rain and shine, and destined for a thousand years more of colorful life there under the turquoise sky.

He turned by the old plinth, stopping to bless himself by tapping his hairy chest with the black manikin, after which he passed firmly to the platform above the plaza, facing the emperor, and announced:

"O Za Ramna, the mighty, by the spirits of thy ancestors, in the halls of Chichen Itza, prepare thy children for the sacrifice! Prepare for the holy visit of the great Sun God!"

The soldiers below—both jaguar and puma—held up their lances, from which the stone tips had been removed in honor of the religious character of the occasion, and sang a mournful dirge, accompanied by drums and flageolets.

Then a solemn hush descended on the throng—and by this time a throng indeed had assembled along all the ways leading to the plaza. Every one in Maya who dared brave the rigors of the Ravine of the Ants and who longed for a sight of the splendors of Chichen Itza had found a chance to see and be seen.

They would wait in the broiling sun as long as necessary, that they might be present in that one brief moment when the Sun Virgin would be lifted by the officiating priests and dropped into the well.

The jaguar skins and puma skins formed a lane, and deflected their glances again lower than ever now.

Through the lane, her head still high, that rapt look of exaltation still alight on her countenance—uplifted as with a spirit such as martyrs only know—such as only the spiritually exalted can understand—on the sacred llama rode Za Chel.

At the foot of the steps of the Sun Temple two priests

stepped forward and took her by the hand and assisted her to alight, but it seemed to the crowd breathlessly watching that she needed no assistance.

Za Chel seemed in a dream, far removed from the world about her. Already in thought she was transported to that far dwelling in the skies which would be hers anon.

Guided by the priests, she started up the steps, but slowly withdrew her hands from theirs and waved them aside. Respectfully they fell back.

ALONE, UNAIDED, SHE mounted, step by step, and disappeared inside the broad columns and was hid from view.

This temple was no different from the one in which she always had lived, which rendered it simple and easy for her to seek the customary robing chamber.

When the Sun Virgin disappeared from view a long gasp escaped the crowd, as if in unison. They knew there must be some delay. She must be prepared properly for the sacrifice.

Yet it was very hot out there in the stone plaza. And a long way back through the barren Ravine of the Ants to the huts of Maya. They were eager to have it over.

Za Ramna mopped his brow. From being very pale his face had suddenly become suffused with a quick color. His blood seemed playing tricks with him.

Meanwhile two priests went to the lip of the well, and parted the vines so as to be sure of a firm foothold; but they moved very gently so as not to disturb the crawling tenants in the depths just below.

The minutes dragged. Za Chel was taking her time in her preparations.

Pocapa Tlal signaled the two slaves who had borne the

head of his litter. They reached within it and brought forth two enormous baskets, filled with the little brown pellets made of chicle, tobacco and cocaine. *Yinska*—which made men as gods, oblivious of the sordid affairs of earth, ecstatic!

Obeying the orders of the High Priest, they passed the *yinska* pellets around the plaza, among the jaguar soldiers.

It was a gracious act of hospitality from the religious to the temporal power—the offering of this sedative, this pellet of forgetfulness to render the rays of the Sun God a little less intense on this scorching day.

As one of the slaves of the High Priest passed near Za Ramna with his open basket, the emperor leaned down and beckoned. The slave lifted up the basket, and the emperor took from it two of the brown pellets and placed them in his capacious mouth. Slowly he masticated the blessed *yinska*.

No one thought of offering a pellet to Za Chel. Was she not favored above all? Was this not to be her day of days? Who else than Za Chel was to be Bride of the Sun?

At length Pocapa Tlal became a little impatient. He turned to find out what could be detaining the Virgin; and at that moment his chief assistant came out from the temple bearing the great emerald of Cochibar.

Pocapa Tlal sent him across the plaza with the jewel to deliver it to the emperor.

Then the High Priest sat down again with reassurance. He was satisfied. If Za Chel had given up the emerald of Cochibar then indeed was she all but ready.

There was left to her now only the royal *huitzin*, and that would slip from her only on the lip of the well—at the supreme moment.

19

BRIDE OF THE SUN

IN THE ROBING chamber of the temple Za Chel reclined on the raised platform, gazing up into the light through the long, narrow aperture which had been left through the roof to admit this scant illumination.

A moment since, she had taken from her bosom the great green jewel of Cochibar and had handed it to one of the women, who, in turn, had taken it to the waiting assistant priest at the farther door, whence it had passed, by customary stages, back to her father, the emperor, on his red throne across the plaza.

That symbolized her farewell to the world—the giving up, voluntarily, of the vanities and beauties and earthly glories of this transitory life.

She was now on the threshold of her immortal life with her celestial bridegroom.

Yet not quite ready. Her slim, lovely body must receive its final deft manipulation at the hands of the experts—for the bridegroom was a jealous god. What else than earth's most exquisite virgin, and in her most elegant perfection, could satisfy his exacting taste?

As Za Chel reclined, the women sponged her body with the sacred water which had been collected from the calyxes of the hibiscus flowers in the hour before dawn; and then kneaded her with the fragrant myrrh and cassia mingled with the oil from the coconut.

After which she came to a sitting posture, while they arranged her black tresses in elaborate waves of an ascending coiffure which was built about a concealed network of rose-colored shell.

Then, from the tiny pots of chalcedony, which had been blessed by the priests, the women removed trifling specks of vermilion and ochre, and began blending the two earthy pigments skillfully into a bright pinkish color that well simulated the rich flow of healthy blood to an excited cheek.

With this cosmetic they anointed the lobes of the ears, the inner nostrils, the lips, and the upper parts of the cheeks. Then they painted little spots of red on the knee caps, and painted every toe nail and every finger nail a vivid vermilion.

This was a ritual, for the Sun Virgin must go to her groom with the vivid glow of life, and—alas!—often she went bloodless at the supreme moment. It even had been known that virgins had fainted before being thrown into the well. The priests explained easily that this was due to the violence of their ecstasy of anticipation for their celestial lover.

Pocapa Tlal had predicted, however, that Za Chel would not faint. She was made of stern fiber, despite the fair curves of her soft, youthful body.

Yet she must be colored. It was the law of sacrifice.

NOW SHE WAS ready for the vestments.

First was the *huipila* of the Virgin. This was no more

than a girdle a few inches wide, tied across the thighs—of snow white, and filmy. It was the only garment she would wear into the presence of the celestial bridegroom.

Next came the jewels of her maidenly but imperial collection. A collar of round green jade, perfectly matched. Twin breastplates of turquoise, shell and carnelian, with two choice pieces of white jade fitted in them. And an armlet of pink chalcedony for each slender wrist. Her coiffure was held in place by a thin band of almost transparent gold.

Finally, when she was quite ready, the *huitzin*, bequeathed from her ancestors, and which she would leave—not to her descendants, but to the progeny of her royal father—was wrapped about her, to be held in place snugly across her slender throat until the supreme moment, on the lip of the well.

In a corner of the chamber had been fitted a huge slab of mica. It was almost perfect, though two wrinkles ran diagonally across its lower part. Though the light was dim, it served as a mirror.

Za Chel stood there for a moment, while the women respectfully remained aside. She looked at herself calmly; then she closed her eyes—for a last secret communing with that red-headed stranger who had preceded her into the land of the sky—and when she opened them it was with a start, for one of the women was plucking the hem of the *huitzin*.

"The High Priest wishes to know how long, O Virgin!"

Gone at once was the inner vision of that stranger.

Slowly she permitted the *huitzin* to open and she took one last look in the mica mirror at the fair loveliness which would soon be offered to the great Sun God. Then she folded the *huitzin* again about her, wrapped herself securely from chin to heels, and calmly said:

"To Pocapa Tlal, greetings! Za Chel is ready!"

Slowly she turned and slowly walked from the chamber. Ahead of her scuttled the tirewoman with the welcome news to the impatient High Priest.

IT WAS JUST past the moment of high noon. For six hours, or a bit longer, the Mayans had been sweltering under the fierce heat of the last moments of summer, for the month of the pestle, known as Mac, was the one which ushered in the fall. It occurred during the equinox, and the day of the sacrifice of the Virgin was always chosen to fall on what would be known in later ages as the 21st of September—when summer met autumn.

The priests had long since fixed this as the day—in ages of Maya long gone. Why they fixed it there no Mayan knew. For the priests were the mouthpieces of the gods, and they had let it be known that the Sun God himself desired this day of the equinox for the reception of his bride.

Nature almost invariably sends a storm at this crux of the seasons, and, as the sacrifice was made solely that rains might proceed, it was a fair prognostication that within a day or two there would be a downpour.

Now, a bit sooner than usual, and rather suddenly, the sky became overcast. A black cloud floated across the face of the sun. Pocapa Tlal saw it was high time to conclude the sacrifice and to do it promptly.

By all known and reasonably exact portents, if the Sun Virgin were given to the Well at once, there might be an immediate reply from Ah Bolan Dzacab. It might rain before night. Again, and most dramatically, would the promise of the priests be fulfilled, before the people.

But beyond the vision of Pocapa Tlal, more than a mile away, a strange apparition was diverting the thought of the farther fringe of Mayans from the great event at the Well.

A strange moving fort was skirting the crowd and bearing as rapidly as possible toward the plaza—though still far too far away to reach it before the ceremony would be over—unless something intervened.

The moving fort was the Norse phalanx—Rorek and his five. He had left the land of the Olmecans, to advance swiftly to the rescue he had planned.

Were this not Chichen Itza—the sacred place, inviolate, apart—the coming of the phalanx would have been known to Pocapa Tlal; but the conch shell telegraph did not work through the Ravine of the Ants.

Therefore the lesser Mayans at the edge of the crowd were the first to know of the formidable coming of the Norsemen. They were panic-stricken by it, but made no resistance. The word trickled on up to the jaguar soldiers, who disbelieved it, for, looking back, they saw nothing.

Rorek and his five had discreetly debouched along a jungle path that would bring them out in the rear of the Sun Temple and to the right of the well.

The jaguar soldiers did not send on the mad rumor. This day was religious, and it was up to the puma-clad troops to maintain order. The tall gods were dead, anyway.

QUITE UNCONSCIOUS OF the little band moving against him, Pocapa Tlal saw the supreme moment had come. He glanced across to Za Ramna, and saw the emperor was sorely in need of retiring to his litter. The stout ruler sagged on the red dais so noticeably that the aid of two slaves was needed to hold him in his imperial place.

Za Ramna had imbibed plentifully of *mishla* along the way, under the cover of the banners of his litter. And then the *yinska* had completed the work. He was already fairly transported beyond the cares of a mundane state.

In a few minutes the Sun Virgin would be cast into the Well—and Za Ramna, the father, and therefore the chief benefactor of his people in offering this choice possession to Ah Bolan Dzacab, would be in his litter, in a drugged, drunken sleep, being borne back to his palace in Uxmal.

Behind the High Priest stood Za Chel, awaiting the final summons. A walk of fifty paces and she would be at the Well.

Pocapa Tlal spoke at last.

"Mayans!" he said. "The supreme moment approaches! Za Ramna, the mighty, ruler of the land, and potentate of the earth, offers his fairest daughter as a bride to the Sun God! Observe—and pray! Pray that with this fair bride the great Sun God, as a nuptial present to the land of Maya, will appease the wrath of Ah Bolan Dzacab, that the rains may come and the land be fructified!"

He waved his manikin, and led the way down the steps of the temple toward the Well.

Ten paces behind came Za Chel, erect, calm.

From beyond the Well came two assisting priests, chosen for their stalwart strength and their firm nerves. Nude, they stood in muscular certainty, grimly observing the soft and measured advance of the feather-clad Virgin.

Not for Pocapa Tlal or his priests was the *yinska* or the *mishla* on that day—not before sundown.

The eyes of the priests were clear; every movement as sure as that of a jaguar stalking an unsuspecting prey in the dim jungle.

On the lip of the Well, Pocapa Tlal paused and turned, waiting until Za Chel should approach. She came within a dozen paces of the yawning black chasm, and, at a gesture from the High Priest, stopped.

Pocapa Tlal then gestured toward her and with a single movement she shed the *huitzin.* It fell rippling to her feet on the broad stone coping.

She stepped forth, toward the Well, clad only in her ornaments and the slender white *huipila.*

Pocapa Tlal lifted up his hands, "O Za Chel!" he cried, "Chief Virgin of the Sun! Unto thee immortal life as the favored bride of the great god!"

Then he reverently bowed his head, Za Chel kept her head up, her eyes closed. Only those nearest could see that the blood seemed gone from her body. Her lips were tightly drawn, and her hands closed, more and more tightly, until the nails cut into the flesh of the palms.

Along the back of her neck, where the cosmetic had not been applied, her olive skin became like wax. The vermil-ion-spots on her knees and cheek bones showed forth poignantly.

Her body swayed, ever so slightly, as if a slight breeze were wafting her too frail corporeal self into the abyss before the ritual could be properly performed.

Pocapa Tlal lifted his head and saw the danger that she

might collapse. She was standing as if in a cataleptic trance; she might have been turned to stone.

The blackness was growing more imminent in the sky. And a fierce murmur was rising from the distant crowds.

"Now!" he ordered swiftly to the naked priestly assistants.

They advanced and seized Za Chel in their firm hands and awaited the word to lift her. She subsided against them like a tired child.

20

CONFLICT

ALMOST AT THE very moment when Pocapa Tlal gave the order to his assistants to seize the Virgin the tropic storm broke. A flash of lightning, a peal of thunder, and then the swift downpour.

The lightning struck the Red Palace, on whose stone steps sat the emperor, and shattered part of the wall. The thunder roused the sodden Za Ramna from his drugged stupor, as a dislodged cracked stone of the broken masonry rolled to his feet. Then his flesh was drenched in rain, and his sorry paunch, fat and feverish, rose and fell greedily under the fresh cool water.

His bleary eyes opened and he looked straight across the plaza to the Well. Forked lightning seemed ripping through his tired brain. The fingers of the devilish *yinska* were tearing at the roots of his nerves. The fiery tongues of the *mishla* were spitting at him from within his skull.

He felt afire, aghast—tortured beyond endurance—and now roused to consciousness by the torrent of water from the skies!

Yet all this was but a hideous background, a crazing nightmare of cruel indecision and of mocking phantoms. There, on the lip of the Well, he saw most clearly—no

phantom this, no dream, no mirage of a sun-baked day—
Za Chel!

Za Chel! The sacred llama of his inner heart. The dear
child whose sweet innocence had slept against his breast.
Favorite daughter of his elder years, sweet solace for his
heavy days. There she stood in her snow-white slender
huipila—on the edge of the sacrificial Well.

Pure, delicate, exalted, chosen flower of the nation!

Yet she was the heart of his heart! That he could offer
her thus on the altar of his gods was the final proof of his
devotion to his people. This was the price he must pay for
his empire. Had not his ancestors, from the time of Ra-Mu,
devotedly given the lives of their best beloved that the
people might live?

Yet there she stood—not yet bestowed to the Well. Frac-
tional seconds had elapsed. He shook his head to throw
off the thick fumes of the *mishla,* to drive down the jagged
crazy forks of lightning from the prodding *yinska.*

Neither alcohol nor cocaine could deaden him. There
she stood—still alive—Za Chel!

For what? Stubbornly, from some yawning pit, deeper
than any well, forgotten in his inner nature, his manhood
was fighting back to life through fateful seconds.

"Za Chel!" the old emperor cried. "For what are you to
be torn from my heart?"

The rain smote him and he tossed his head valiantly,
gazing for a second, straight into the livid heavens, fighting
with his last ounce of strength for some fugitive thought
which eluded him crazily there in the background of that
dancing army of cruel devils taunting him within his brain.

Then, as he saw the priests look to Pocapa Tlal for the

final word, he felt as if his brain had been stricken as had been the stone plinth a moment since. Light swept through him.

Za Chel was being offered to the Well that Ah Bolan Dzacab might send rain to the people. And the rain had come! The rain had come!

What a travesty! What a mockery of life! That he, the emperor, heir of Ra-Mu, the sole will of a mighty people, omnipotent in Maya, should give the life of his chiefly beloved—for what?

For something his people already had!

THERE REMAINED BARE seconds in which to act. It might even now be too late, for there Pocapa Tlal turned his obese stomach toward the Well and made as if about to utter the final word.

In despair, but with imperial strength, Za Ramna lifted his hand to his throbbing brow, as he rose, and cried, piercingly:

"Halt! Pocapa Thal!"

As his hand touched his brow in the hope of relieving the pain it came in contact with the great green emerald of Cochibar, placed there but a moment since, after lying all day on the fair breast of Za Chel. And when his hand came down, impatiently, the thin gold thread broke and there, in his palm, lay the jewel, the size of an egg—and heavy.

Now he was running pell-mell down the steps of the Red Palace, toward the Well, the emerald clutched in his hand. As he ran he yelled, "Stop!"

The method was not imperial. It was devoid of beauty or grace or dignity. It was the most extraordinary thing that had ever been known in all the history of Maya. The soldiers stood as if rooted, in consternation. The vast crowds gaped at this imperial cataclysm. Za Ramna running to the Well—when all knew that only the High Priest might stand there at this supreme moment.

Pocapa Tlal quickly and shrewdly saw that he must at once capitalize this sudden rain. The Virgin must be cast into the Well, so that all the people could see that thus the gods had been propitiated, so that the mouthpiece of the gods might prosper.

To save Za Chel now might imperil the whole religious structure of Maya. One more step forward and the religious order could rule Maya—with the emperor tottering as he was; but one step back and the priesthood might itself tumble into ruin.

Swiftly he gave the order to his two stout assistants: "The bridegroom calls for—"

Even as he spoke, and more swiftly than moved his tongue, the right arm of Za Ramna flew back, and from his fist was hurled the great emerald of Cochibar—full fair across half the plaza, whence he was stumbling now in his aroused zeal to avert the doom so near Za Chel.

The emerald struck the first priest, whose hand was about to lift up the Virgin, fair in the eye. Then it rolled sharply to the feet of Pocapa Tlal.

The High Priest stooped to pick up the stone—for even in that moment his greed was uppermost—and as he stooped the second priest called gruffly to the first:

"Take hold of her! And up with her!"

But the first was moaning with pain from his bruised eye, and now the emperor himself was very near—so near the second priest hesitated to change the ritual alone and complete the act which required the services of two.

Seeing the difficulty, Pocapa Tlal waddled forward to perform the act of throwing in the bride himself, but, as his hand touched the bare shoulder of the still entranced Za Chel, a mighty palm, though shaking as with palsy, was laid upon him, and he was twisted rudely about to face a ruler flaring at last into imperial potency.

"How dare you, Pocapa? Do you hear your emperor?"

"How dare *you*, Za Ramna? Do you hear the voice of the gods?"

"Aye—the voice of my ancestor, Ra-Mu, and of the father god, It Zamna!"

Pocapa Tlal opened his mouth in awe, and not a little fear.

Za Ramna smote his breast wildly. His hands were clenching and unclenching. His features were working with nervous twitchings, and his vast stomach, unused to exertion, was heaving violently.

"It Zamna!" he gasped. "Commands—commands—"

He leaned ponderously on the shaggy breast of the High Priest. Pocapa Tlal impatiently thrust his emperor off. "The *yinska* has destroyed your senses!" he exploded venomously.

LESS THAN A minute had elapsed since the arrival of Za Ramna at the lip of the Well, and now Za Chel came from her strange exalted condition—the cataleptic trance which providentially had intervened to spare her the physical agony she must face in the viperish depths of the murky Well below.

There was her father only a step away—or was it her father? Was she still in the world she knew?

She reached forth her hands and felt for him, like a somnambulist, and as her tiny fingers touched him she woke to the reality and collapsed—on his breast. He gathered her there, in his voluminous embrace, and the tears rolled down his cheeks. He sobbed so loudly all could hear.

Even at that moment the rain ceased.

Pocapa Tlal rudely parted the imperial pair, father and daughter.

"It is time!" he rudely ordered.

"Time?" Za Ramna, for the first time in years, rose to his full height. Full well he believed that It Zamna, the father god, and Ra-Mu, his ancestor, were speaking through him. "Your time, Pocapa Tlal, has come! Prepare!"

Then with infinite tenderness he embraced Za Chel and kissed her forehead just below the hair, where the cosmetic had not been placed.

She was quite herself now and looked at him, wonderingly. She had been rudely seized from her exalted self-hypnosis wherein she was imaginatively ascending the nuptial couch of the Sun God. Awake, on earth, she was still in a daze.

"Za Chel!" he murmured softly in the faintest whisper. "My dear!"

And then he slipped down on the stone at her feet, on the very lip of the Well. Physically a somewhat ugly object, in his obesity, he sprawled out negligently and was at rest.

21

AN EMPIRE WITHOUT A HEAD

THERE WAS BUT one will in Maya—and that lay supine. Pocapa Tlal hesitated an instant—and as he hesitated a warning call from his chief assistant directed his glance to the west end of the Sun Temple, a bare hundred yards away.

What he saw paralyzed his tongue. For now he knew that his craven puma soldiers had not burned the giant sailors from the far ocean on the pyre of their swanlike boat.

He saw the Norse phalanx coming and, at its head, the flaming poll of that impudent stranger who had broken in Pocapa Tlal's own hand his first *pecate*.

Rorek and his five had skirted the crowd, their presence disbelieved by the soldiers, and had come to the vicinity of the Well from the jungle side, where no Mayans were and, therefore, no guards.

Pocapa Tlal's first instinct was to protect the person of the Virgin from profane sight and touch. This audacious stranger had once penetrated to her sleeping chamber. What might he not dare now?

Speaking quickly to his two assistants Pocapa Tlal wrapped the *huitzin* protectingly about Za Chel and, guarded by the two executioners, scuttled with her rapidly to a little door which was hidden in the side of the steps of the Sun Temple.

There the priests and Za Chel disappeared, in full sight of Rorek and the archers, but without the Mayans realizing what was happening.

Rorek dashed for the little door, only to find it closed tight. Vainly he pounded and struck on it with the hilt of his sword. It was of stone.

Rorek turned back to go around up the front steps of the temple in full sight of the crowd, but to do so, he was obliged to pass near the mouth of the Well. Already the cotton soldiers were assembling there, led by their commander, the ambitious little Princess Taycapin.

As Rorek came toward them, their ranks parted and Taycapin stood forth. She held forth her hand in salute. "Hail!" she cried. "Hail, Quetzalcoatl!"

Then he saw, just beyond her, the supine form of Za Ramna. He went to it quickly and looked down. The body had been turned over and lay on its back.

For just a moment, even in his haste and bewilderment, Rorek was held by the subtle and arresting sight. The imperial face of the ruler who had befriended him seemed changing. The fleshy look—the let-down aspect that came from eating and drinking—seemed to be going.

Across the brows—broad and beautiful in contour now they seemed—a soft glow was settling, such a glow, as comes into the sky at sunset following a storm.

The nose, aquiline, firmly chiseled, the strong beak of a race of conquerors, began to stand out like a command. The mouth below was gaining strength as the heavy jowls became set.

The hazel eyes stared wide open.

Eric muttered: "He's drunk."

Rorek leaned swiftly down, placed an arm under the heavy body to lift it, and then changed his mind. He rose reverently, and bowed his head, as he said simply: "He is dead!"

Taycapin, at his side, added, for his special benefit: "It is the end of a dynasty. Not you, nor I, but the gods have willed it!"

Rorek looked at her and saw that resolute tilt of the ambitious head, that beady glance of the black, narrow eyes, the stern thrust of the bold jaw and the tight lips of the hard mouth—a feminine miniature of all the angular aspects of the dead brother so well buried in rotundity and indulgence.

She thought she saw sympathy in the Norseman's glance, and strove to increase it by crying again, even louder: "Quetzalcoatl!"

ROREK, THE TALENTS that made him a leader highly keyed up, felt the name spread among the cotton soldiers, and even was aware that it was being passed, by devious and swift word of mouth, from the pumas to the jaguars and so to the Mayan masses.

The thousands were agog with wonder and report. It was said the emperor was dead. It was said that Ah Bolan Dzacab had refused to have Za Chel sacrificed, that he had sent the rain in advance to prove his good intent. It was said that the Plumed Serpent had risen from the pyre of his great vessel—a phoenix come to bless Maya in adversity.

Meanwhile all soldiers—the jaguars, the pumas, the cotton wearers—waited forlornly. To them this was chaos.

If Za Ramna was dead, who could give them orders? If Pocapa Tlal was gone—and they could not see him—what should they do?

Rorek was alert and eager, though as yet not committing himself. He had but one thought—to find Za Chel. Yet Taycapin thought even more swiftly. She stepped so closely to him that none could hear, neither his archers, nor her cotton soldiers.

"Your opportunity is divine," she said softly, her eyes becoming languorous as she almost touched him. "Seize it, my friend."

"Where have they taken Za Chel?" Rorek asked.

She stamped her foot abruptly. "You are the Plumed Serpent," she insisted. "Act like one—with divine, swift wisdom. And all Maya is yours." He regarded her gravely, without reply.

"Za Ramna is gone. There is no heir. The throne is yours—for none but a divinity may sit there. Claim it!"

She turned and pointed regally to the red dais on the palace steps across the plaza. "There—where the emperors of Maya have been crowned for more than a thousand years!"

Her hands sought his tunic. Her lashes fell over her black eyes. She leaned her head toward his breast. "And I will be thy empress!"

His reply was cold and direct. "How can I reach Za Chel?" he asked.

"She has gone to her bridegroom, the Sun God!" Taycapin replied, almost insolently, into his face.

Then he seized her angrily by her small wrists. "Tell me,"

he demanded, "how to get into the temple, or by Thor, I will feed *you* to the Well myself!"

Taycapin, in deadly fear of his strength—for her wrists were almost crushed in his unconscious grasp—and abashed by the wild purpose in his livid face, cried, in surprised frankness: "By the front door, to the right of the jaguar column."

He dropped her wrists. She rubbed them with relief, a little surprised to find they were not broken.

Now he acted more swiftly than even she could think. "Eric!" he called.

"Aye, Rorek!"

"Here! You and Hemnet!"

The two archers came at once. Rorek thrust Taycapin toward them, and Eric caught her, enfolded as she was in her voluminous *huitzin*.

"Hold her—against my return!" Hemnet closed in on her farther side. "Do not permit her to escape!"

"Aye, Rorek!" The two looked down on Taycapin, suddenly roused to calm, intense fury, but so startled she had not found the voice to protest.

Then the son of Ha-Aton called, sharply: "Donal! Olav! Galko!" and the three responded. "Come!"

With a bound Rorek, followed by the three, went swiftly up the front steps of the temple.

AS ROREK DISAPPEARED behind the jaguar column of the yellow door above, Taycapin said to Eric and Hemnet: "Unhand me or I will call my soldiers to fire on you."

Hemnet looked to Eric; Eric to Hemnet. Across the head of the tiny woman Hemnet muttered: "Remember Wolfkin."

Around his neck Eric was wearing a hemp scarf given him by an Olmecan girl. He unwound this, and, before Taycapin could guess his purpose, had thrown it about her lower face, and had wound it tightly, tying it behind her head with a knot.

She screamed, but her cry was muffled.

"That will hold her!" Eric said, and then added, in quick consternation: "Help me, Hemnet, she's slippery as a snake!"

So she was, and determined to get away from her huge guards. Wild, desperate in Eric's arms as he held her, she clawed and scratched until the blood ran down his bronzed cheeks.

Then, suddenly, Eric stood there holding the royal *huitzin*—without its contents.

They were standing only a few paces from the lip of the Well and as Hemnet reached for her struggling form, Taycapin sprang away to avoid him. With her *huitzin* gone, she was clothed as had been Za Chel for the sacrifice—in a narrow *huipila* and her rare ornaments.

Free, she tore at the hemp gag across her mouth and lifted it over her head, but, to get it off, she had to draw it over her eyes. At the same time she dodged to escape the clumsy Hemnet, who was closing in on her as a lion might close on a mouse.

For a brief moment her eyesight was blotted out by the scarf, and she did not see the lush vine on the lip of the Well which her foot squashed upon. She slipped.

The next instant she plunged headlong into the Well.

The screams of the descending Taycapin were lost in the

gasps of astonishment that poured from the Mayans, both soldiers and laymen from the plaza and beyond.

Superstitious, believing that each event which occurred came about solely through the will of the gods, they accepted this offer of a victim to the Well as the proper culmination of a day devoted to sacrifice.

The rumor began spreading that it was Za Chel who had been thrown to Ah Bolan Dzacab. So many believed.

22

MAN OF DESTINY

POCAPA TLAL WAS not a man of action. Like his people, he was not essentially warlike, accustomed to having his authority prevail without argument; and he had already lost out in his first meeting with Rorek.

Now he followed the line of his instinct and training and retired at once to the sacred dark place within the great Yellow Temple to think out what to do. Presently he would emerge with a message from the gods, and tell the army and the people how to meet this crisis. Outside in the plaza they were dutifully waiting for his inspired word.

But the mouthpiece of the gods had to get his message first. He was engaged in this highly essential requisite of his calling, kneeling by the sacred flame of the eternal charcoal brazier, when he was rudely bowled over and his breath nearly knocked from his heavy, and bewildered body.

He picked himself up, to face the drawn iron dagger of Rorek, that same dagger which had smashed his *pecate*. The High Priest looked up in amazed horror at that set, desperate face behind bristling red whiskers.

"Where is Za Chel?"

"The Virgin is sacred—" The fat, hairy hands, so adept

at plucking living hearts from bound beasts, were held up in horror.

"I want her!"

"But—"

"Speak!"

Pocapa felt the gaunt long Norse fingers in his soft throat; felt them close about his wide gullet; felt his knees knocking in despair. Then his breath was gone. He could not utter a word. He collapsed.

With a fierce imprecation Rorek dropped him and turned to the next room. There, facing him, arms crossed, stood the two naked executioners.

Sensing that the object of his quest was very near, frantic with fear that harm had come to her, Rorek leaped on these two stalwarts of Maya, who still were undersized before his virile youth and height.

They were quite unprepared for this totally unexpected and astounding attack. In their memory or in all the legends of Maya, no one had ever so daringly entered a Mayan temple before—certainly not in the very presence of the High Priest.

With almost a single sweep of his arms and fists, Rorek hurled them to the stone floor, tumbling them beside their half unconscious master.

Behind him entered Donal, Galko, and the ox-like Olav, with drawn swords, ready to kill at a word or a look from Rorek.

"Guard them! Don't let them move!" roared the red-haired leader, pointing to the three Mayan dignitaries. "Hold your knives to their throats. If I find she has been harmed—*ssst!*" He drew his hand across his jugular; and was gone.

Pocapa Tlal came to a sitting posture, and, as he tried to rise, felt the sword point of Galko in his abdomen. He began talking, volubly. There was no answer. He called to his two assistants. They responded from a few feet away, on the floor at his side.

The High Priest looked. There lay his best men—even as he lay—an inch from naked Norse blades.

For a long time they lay there; very, very quietly and uncomfortably.

IN THE DIMLY lit stone chamber deeper in the temple, Za Chel, wrapped in her *huitzin*, huddled forlorn and bewildered on the raised platform. She had been looking on the broad bare backs of the two priests who a moment since had her there by the Well. Would they soon take her thither again? Trembling, miserable, she was only upbraiding herself for her fears. Would the gods help her? For in her frail mortal weakness, she was now fearing the Well— she was horribly afraid she would break down and reveal herself as some common maiden and not the imperial daughter of the royal divine house of Ramna.

Then some ruffian seized the two officiating priests, and in a twinkling they were dashed from her sight. The next moment she was gazing into the blue eyes—the red hair—of the tall stranger.

Had her trance returned? The blessed trance! Was she in that drugged ecstasy where went only mortal eaters of *yinska* and immortal brides of the sun?

She gasped. She scarcely breathed, in her wonder.

"Za Chel!" he softly whispered.

"Aye!"

"Are you harmed?"

"No, my Lord!"

"Thank Wodin!"

Devoutly, with a terrific relief, he sat beside her.

As she had once in that far distant night, she reached forth her little hand and timidly touched his bare arm, and then withdrew her hand quickly.

He was alive. It shocked her.

In a brief moment his relaxation was over. Now he must act. He reached forth and lifted her in his arm, cupping it about her and drawing her up level to his breast. Strength flowed into him; new purpose.

What else could divinity be, thought Za Chel, than this? Old ideas came back to her, the full force of her training and her ancestry. With her two hands she held him off, startled at first, and then half frightened.

"Please!" she implored.

"But I have come—come for you—to rescue you, take you from here. We will fly to the hills—to my Olmecans—and be safe." He bowed his head, ever so slightly. "I love you, Za Chel. Thought of you possesses me, night and clay."

Her little hands wavered at this, fluttering over his hairy tunic, and withdrawing. Timid—yet not too timid. Attracted. Then repelled.

"No," she said softly, though her eyes were filled with a tender glamour—the far suggestion of dreaming moonlight, of a vast longing for something that could never be. "No!"

"But why?"

"I could never leave Maya!"

"You will die here!"

"I am the Bride of the Sun God!"

She said it so simply, so finally that it had more effect with him than any words ever spoken.

Something vast and elemental, daring and profound, was kindled in him. It was as if a great machine lay dead and one touched a button and it sprang to life—instantly, in all its complex and intricate skill and beauty.

What he had vaguely planned, what he had half prom-ised his loyal archers, what had been demanded by the audacity of Taycapin, were as tinder and flint lying dormant in his dynamic spirit for that one spark that could be struck only by Za Chel—and without any intent on her part!

THERE YET WAS time neither for talk nor question. The day was slipping into the west. Those masses in the plaza beyond the heavy doors of the temple, bewildered, meek, must have some master—and promptly.

In the opening and closing of Za Chel's eyes he grew to imperial stature. He grew like that, amazingly, achieving all his latent possibilities.

"Come!" he said, simply, reaching out his arm.

She hesitated, so he calmly took her and carried her to where the three archers stood above the three priests.

"Quick! Bind them!" he commanded. His Norsemen obeyed.

Pocapa Tlal protested, and when no notice was taken of his words, he started to call for his soldiers. But the thick walls deadened his voice. No one knew better than he how improbable it was that a cry from within the Yellow Temple could be heard outside.

Rorek said to Galko: "Run to the Well and bring that cloak worn by the emperor—and bring Eric and Hemhet, with the woman!"

While they were gone Za Chel looked up at him and said, with quiet dignity: "My Lord, where is my father?"

"Dead, my dear!"

She gasped, drew in her breath and looked at him, wide-eyed.

He placed an arm about her. "But I am here!"

She drew toward him more gently and said softly: "I fear—I am afraid and know not what to do!"

He held her close. "I know!" he answered—and waited, in silence, while the three priests glared at him.

Shortly Eric came in, bearing the *huitzin* of Za Ramna, which he handed to Rorek.

"That woman is gone, chief!" blurted out Eric shame-facedly.

"Gone! What do you mean?"

"She slipped from me like an eel, chief—and then, as Hemnet reached for her, she slipped into the Well."

A slow ironic smile spread over Rorek's features. "It is time!" he said, reaching for the hand of Za Chel.

IN THE PLAZA the mass of soldiers and of Mayans were mingling in confusion. All eyes dwelt on the closed doors of the Yellow Palace of the Sun. Thence must issue the next authority, for by now they knew that the emperor was dead.

What would it be? Without male issue who would reign? As by immemorial custom the High Priest would have much to say—unless the gods spoke clearly, by unmistakable sign, without him.

The yellow door above swung slowly outward, and there,

on the upper step, appeared five archers—Eric, leading the way stalwartly, sword in hand, buckler on arm. The other four came two abreast, following. Donal and Galko, Olav and Hemnet—swords elevated, bucklers held high.

A thrilling sight. Such simple military strength so fearless before those hordes. They marched slowly, majestically, to the bottom of the steps, where Eric cleared a space, without a word, by exercising his long sword.

Then Eric turned and spoke sharply—in Norse, which was incomprehensible and therefore divine to the simple, ignorant Mayans who listened.

"Up with the bucklers!" he cried.

As one the five shields rose aloft, over the heads of the archers.

"Fix the thwart clasps!" Eric commanded.

With a rattle and snap the five were fastened securely. Some who had seen the raising of the buckler throne at Mayapan and Uxmal knew what it meant and whispered avidly to their neighbors. An awed murmur ran through the populace. This was the kingly seat of the flaming-haired stranger, already acknowledged by Za Ramna and Pocapa Tlal as visiting royalty from the mysterious eastern sea. Awe and respect seized the crowd.

Then through the doors above came Rorek himself. And by his side walked Za Chel, whom many thought to have been already the Sun God's bride.

A sigh of wonder and a murmur of holy awe spread everywhere, for the red-haired stranger came not in hairy tunic and naked arms and legs as before, but clothed now in the soft feathery folds of the *huitzin*. The royal mantle of Za Ramna hung majestically from his neck, and gave

back subtly and with ever-spreading beauty the splendor
and diversity of the sun.

As all well knew, no one not royal and divine could wear
the *huitzin* and live!

Za Chel, in her feathery robe, walked not as she had
when with her father in her earlier years, at the rear—for
now she was at the side of the oncoming Norseman.

When Rorek came to the next to the bottom step he
reached down, placed an arm about Za Chel, lifted her,
and, with one easy spring, leaped to the buckler throne.

There he placed her gently on her feet, drew forth his
long sword, elevated it, and cried in mighty tones: "On!"

The five split the welkin with their hail to the acknowledged chief, while the Mayans watched with a slow beginning of comprehension. They were to have a new ruler.

Across the plaza, imperially, the buckler throne was
borne, from the Yellow Temple of the Sun to the Red
Palace of the Emperor.

Arrived at the foot of the steps of the Red Palace, Rorek
leaped from the buckler throne to the steps, assisted Za
Chel to his side, and slowly began the ascent.

He reached the dais of red porphyry—the throne of
Maya—and turned to face the vast throng. The jaguar
and puma soldiers below looked up appalled. The Mayan
masses looked on dumbly. Many were uplifted with a
portent of good fortune, for, at that moment, the sun broke
through a cloud and his rays fell on the soft folds of the
royal *huitzin* and made it glow with gleaming color.

Rorek raised his hand. "Mayans!" he called in tones that
no puny Mayan could match.

Silence reigned, while his archers stood below, stoutly waiting behind their great bucklers.

Then through the silence a Mayan voice rang. It was that of the captain of the guard of Za Ramna. He had sensed what was to happen, and thought to be the first to greet the rising sun of coming favor.

"Listen to the wisdom of the Plumed Serpent!" he cried.

Rorek calmly continued, to an ever-rising fever of acclaim: "I, Quetzalcoatl, come to you as a new ruler from beyond the seas—out of the foam of the great eastern waters—to be your emperor. Here, in the sight of gods and men, I promise to rule all without fear or favor, for the good of Maya!"

As the ripple of wondering approval spread he held up his hand for further silence.

"Here!" he said, placing a hand on the arm of Za Chel, "is the daughter of Za Ramna, bride of your new emperor."

So Quetzalcoatl came to his throne.

In Maya many said that Za Chel, in very truth, became the Bride of the Sun. Had they not seen her leap into the Well? She must have been taken thence and given by her august master to his flaming-haired vice-regent upon earth, the mighty Quetzalcoatl.

EPILOGUE

SUCH IS THE story told me in the hut by the banks of the river in Yucatan by the Guarani, whose wife was descended from the Mayan keeper of the public granary in the lost city of Ixamal—the city that has never been found, so deep has the jungle grown above it.

I returned to the hotel in Belize to write it down, that it might live for all to know the wonder of a day long gone.

In that Honduran hotel I met an American archaeologist, who was greatly interested in the Guarani's story. He took from his bag of specimens a square stone—about eight inches each way. It was intricately carved and excited my interest.

"I picked this up in Mitla, the old capital of the Toltecs," said the professor. "It has to do with the reign of Quetzalcoatl. See, here is the date. Year 40 of the Third Dynasty, which it is known was founded by Quetzalcoatl."

"What year would that be in our time?"

"About 1146 A.D. Now, in that corner of it is a curious glyph, or inscription. That, we have decided, indicates an important crisis in Mayan history. It indicates the League of Mayapan, when church and state were joined by Quetzalcoatl, to the benefit of the state and the subjugation of the church.

"See above—that transverse glyph with the arrow. That stands for Quetzalcoatl as a Toltec noble. But here, just below, he stands as an Olmecan chieftain. And here he stands as Emperor of Maya. And there, in that corner, with that little curlicue which is the sea, he is a stranger from beyond the ocean. A complex character, what?"

"Just as the Guarani pictured him," I observed.

"The deeper I get into the Mayan record, the more I become convinced that Quetzalcoatl was the greatest man that ever appeared in Central America," the professor continued. "It is certain he is the man who put an end to the practice of human sacrifice, though the Aztecs, to the north, later revived it for a time. It is also certain that he broke the people from slavish bondage to an imperial idea. He was also an artist, a great hunter and a mighty builder. He built the wonderful serpent columns at Castillo, and a dozen or more cities besides after his people were obliged to leave Maya."

In the center of the stone was a circular plaque, about an inch and a half in diameter. On it was graven an intaglio of two heads. I asked about them.

"Those are portraits of Quetzalcoatl and his empress," said the professor, "and for that reason this stone is extremely rare. I know of no other instance in Mayan carvings in which a ruler is shown with a consort; but you can see the second head is that of a woman, and of a different bone structure.

"Now study those two heads. An observing artist did them. See, the man's has a high frontal bone, and the hair falls back as if it were silky. Take this magnifying glass and you can detect embedded in the hair a fleck of red mica. That means he was red-haired. Even if the glyph were not there, we would know that was Quetzalcoatl. And now study the woman, with the slight Mongoloid tilt to the eyebrows and more wiry hair. A different race. Yet consorts, a most significant fact, as you will agree."

I turned to the scholar. "You say you find no other instances of ruler and consort together in Mayan sculpture?"

"None," he assured me, "which leads us to believe that another of the distinctions of Quetzalcoatl was that in an age in which woman was little more than a beast of burden and an object of human sacrifice, he was the first to lift her to a seat with the mighty."

"Does this glyph say that is Za Chel?"

"Exactly; and I rather fancy the old red-head was rather fond of her, in his way!"

"That is what the Guarani told me," I replied.

ABOUT THE AUTHOR

WHO'S WHO IN AMERICA describes Richard Barry as an author, and lists among his works published novels, produced plays, and a long series of experiences as a newspaper and magazine correspondent. It does not list him among the heat manufacturers, for, though he was born in Wisconsin where the thermometer goes to forty below on occasion, he usually spends his winters in southern California, where, at the base of Mount Wilson, he has a hillside lookout surveying seven cities and Catalina Island. Summers he comes to Westchester County, where he has an old stone barn just beyond the New York City line. There he has a little theater in the wagon shed and tries out his plays as well as those of neighbors who write them. This winter he is a photo dramatist for Fox talking pictures.

Barry has been in every important country on the five continents and in each State of the Union. When he goes from New York to California he drives his own car. He does not like short motor trips—nothing under three thousand miles. But he takes these easily, stops off a good deal, meets the local people and thus is constantly in touch with refreshing "atmosphere." After six months of intensive writing he finds that three weeks of motoring tunes him up for another six months and brings a new supply of ideas.

His hobbies are his wife, his dog, his garden and his automobile. His religion is Outofdoors. His clubs include the Ancient Order of Coast to Coasters, and the Heirs of the Covered Wagon. He had a medal once from an emperor. His wife found it the other day in an old trunk.

He thinks the first law of man is to write, and that the way to learn to write is by writing. But he does not believe in too intense a specialization in writing. After he prepares a special article for a magazine, he thinks that helps him to start plotting and constructing a play. After depicting the characters of the play, through dialogue alone, he feels better able to go at the narrative writing of a serial novel. After the extended concentration required for a novel he finds a snappy relief in a short story. He has written eight serials and many shorter stories for *Argosy*.